WAITING FOR AQUARIUS
and other columns

WAITING FOR AQUARIUS
and other columns

by **John Levesque**

Mosaic Press
Oakville-New York-London

CANADIAN CATALOGUING IN PUBLICATION DATA

Levesque, John, 1953-
Waiting for Aquarius & Other Columns
Columns from The Hamilton Spectator

ISBN 0-88962-537-9

I. Title.

PS8573.E84W3 1992 C813'.54 C92-095766-8
PR9199.3.L48W3 1992

Published by MOSAIC PRESS, P.O. Box 1032 Oakville, Ontario, L6J 5E9, Canada. Offices and warehouse at 1252 Speers Road, Units #1&2, Oakville, Ontario, L6L 5N9, Canada.

Mosaic Press acknowledges the assistance of the Canada Council and the Ontario Arts Council in support of its publishing programme.

Design by Patty Gallinger
Front cover photograph by Gary Yokoyama
Typeset by Jackie Ernst

Printed and Bound in Canada.
Second Printing 1993

ISBN 0-88962-537-9 PB

MOSAIC PRESS:
In Canada:
MOSAIC PRESS, 1252 Speers Road, Units 1&2, Oakville, Ontario, L6L 5N9, Canada. P.O. Box 1032, Oakville, Ontario L6J 5E9
In the U.K.:
John Calder (Publishers) Ltd., 9-15 Neal Street, London, WCZH 9TU, England.

For Mon Oncle Jean
and Arthur Parke,
who both loved to laugh

ACKNOWLEDGEMENTS

Many thanks to the editors at the *Hamilton Spectator* who wrestled with my copy over the past decade and always generously gave me enough rope to hang myself: Bas Korstanje, Bill Johnston, Kate Taylor and Dan Kislenko.

Thanks also to Howard Aster at Mosaic Press, who suggested this book, Suzanne Muir, who graciously undertook the awesome chore of typing the manuscript, and Gary Yokoyama, who shot the swell photograph on the cover.

Finally, thanks to the readers who stuck with me through the years, Renee, Christina, family and friends for providing me with an abundance of source material, and the world as a whole for being such a rich and wondrous absurdity. When you get right down to it, we're all waiting for Aquarius.

TABLE OF CONTENTS

1.

IN THE BEGINNING WAS THE WORD

OUT OF THE MOUTH OF ASTRONAUTS

"It's really discouraging to get monkey feces in the cockpit."
-Bob Overmyer

Space shuttle commander Bob Overmyer is probably grateful he wasn't doing anything particularly historic last week when he uttered this thought from space. Still, the intrepid astronaut was speaking for a lot of us when he said it.

Commander Overmyer's eloquent plaint has countless potential applications. "Monkey feces in the cockpit" could eventually enter the language as the universal phrase to indicate that things aren't going quite as smoothly as they could.

Compare the Overmyer quote with Neil Armstrong's platitudinous pronouncement of 1969, upon setting foot on the moon. Mr. Armstrong's "One small step for a man, etc." obviously has limited use in everyday conversation.

Commander Overmyer's words convey a simple, ineffable truth: it *would* be discouraging to get monkey feces in the cockpit, just as it would be discouraging if a faulty hose sprayed urine into the weightless environment of a spacecraft. (This happened too – on the same mission).

And yet, you just know Commander Overmyer's words won't make it into any book of quotations. Only quotations that sound like quotations end up in books of quotations. The quotations that are most quoted are routinely ignored by everyone but the people who compiled them.

For example, you won't find "nice weather ... for ducks" in a book of quotations, even though you hear someone say it just about every time it rains.

How about "that's for me to know, and you to find out"? Thousands of people use that handy little phrase, yet no one knows who coined it, when and under what circumstances. Meanwhile, under the word 'know', we have John Keats on page 383 of *Bartlett's Familiar Quotations* stating "We know her woof, her texture ...", which appears to be an obscure poetic allusion, possibly to someone's dog.

On the subject of monkeys, one of the most popular rejoinders– at least where I grew up – is "I don't make monkeys, I buy them." Do you think I can find out who invented that phrase? Instead, under 'monkey', I am given a quote from Kenneth Grahame: "Monkeys, who very sensibly refrain from speech, lest they should be set to earn their livings." It's clever, though ungrammatical. But I've never heard anyone else say it.

"You and whose army?" is another immensely popular quote whose origin is absent from the annals of popular wisdom, as is "say it, don't spray it."

We all remember what Stanley uttered to Livingstone in darkest Africa, but nobody knows who first said "it's so hot you could fry an egg on the sidewalk."

Shakespeare's best lines are immortal, while the author of "that's so funny I forgot to laugh" remains uncredited.

Why is this? Are the more common examples of popular talk too low-brow for the quotation books? Must the quotations be archaic and out of use to qualify for inclusion?

Christopher Morley, in his preface to the 11th edition of *Bartlett's Quotations*, explains how quotations are selected: "We have found that the images which sink deepest are often those we scarcely knew, at the time, we were noticing at all."

But the truth gives the lie to Mr. Morley's method. Like Commander Overmyer's sagacious observation on monkey feces, the most clever things people say to each other on a daily basis go unrecorded. "Enough white stuff for ya?" is ignored, as is "look up look down, your pants are falling down."

Some scintillating rejoinders such as "sorry about that, chief" are traceable thanks to TV technology. But most of what we hear– and borrow–from others is eventually erased from the collective memory. Meanwhile, marginal quotes from literary figures and others are immortalized.

The only solution is for the average person to be more selective than the quotation-book editors. Or, as the now-legendary Commander Overmyer said about the monkey feces floating in his cockpit: "Don't pick anything out of the air and eat it."

(May 8, 1985)

I'LL TRY TO BE BRIEF

More than a year ago, in a fit of spontaneous generosity, my father-in-law gave me a gift subscription to a popular little magazine that runs condensed versions of stories that have previously run in other periodicals, plus anecdotes of military humour and a condensed book section.

I shan't name the magazine, but roughly one out of every three waiting rooms in this country currently contains the February issue, which features a "Drama In Real Life" about a Norwegian who almost drowned in the North Atlantic.

The enduring appeal of this magazine, I believe, is its brevity. Everybody knows Tolstoy wrote fine novels, but who in his right mind would want to read the whole thing–especially while waiting to have root-canal work done?

The people who publish this magazine swear by the virtues of brevity. Not too long ago, they published a condensed version of the Bible. Many people bought it, perhaps on the assumption that they could find salvation in their spare time.

Nobody made much of a fuss about abridging the Good Book, but I had a vivid picture in my mind of some copy editor nervously drawing huge 'X's over paragraph after paragraph of Scripture, waiting for the skies to part with a mighty blast of thunder as Providence edited him out of the great book of life.

But brevity does have an overwhelming appeal. I attribute the bulk of my not very bulky knowledge of English literature to the people who publish *Coles Notes*, which offers handy outlines of novels in the guise of study booklets.

If, when I was in school, I grew tired of Dickens' exhaustive descriptive passages–which I invariably did–I merely abandoned the book and bought the *Coles Notes*. After all, the people in Dickens' day read his work in serial form and perhaps were lucky enough to be out of town when the boring segments were published.

I, on the other hand, was forced to digest *David Copperfield* over the course of a weekend prior to an exam. A few of my school friends, who found even *Coles Notes* impossibly verbose, did me one better: They based entire secondary-school exam answers on the *Classics Illustrated* comic-book version of the book they were supposed to have read.

Granted, these comic books tended to simplify the story. (Notice how they stayed away from adapting Proust or Joyce.) But a sufficiently motivated student could embroider the story fairly safely, divining the good guys from the bad guys and taking it from there.

Eventually, the conventional wisdom became that brevity needn't take anything away from the idea. In fact, brevity might help distil the idea or at least boil it down until nothing but steam was left.

To this day, I believe the main appeal of Kurt Vonnegut, as a writer, is that he puts asterisks between just about every paragraph in his novels.

***

These gaps give the readers a chance to stop reading pretty well whenever they want.

***

See what I mean?

Brevity is the name of the game these days. The TV networks give us evening "newsbreaks" that come and go in the blink of an eye. Rarely do you see a 60-second commercial on television anymore. Too long. Grammar also waste of time. Fast food , while U wait, drive-in funeral homes, instant breakfast – about the only thing in life that isn't brief is a government brief. But governments are the exception to every rule.

(For a condensed reading of this column, skip paragraphs 1 through 14.)

(March 14, 1984)

OUTWARD AND VISIBLE SIGNS

Language is a rich and organic thing. As with other rich and organic things, people often spread horse manure over it in the mistaken belief that the subsequent harvest will be even richer.

What separates language from other organic things is that it does not suffer horse-manure gladly. When a bureaucrat unearths a term such as "negative growth," you can smell the natural fertilizer he's been using, but you know the soil he's standing on is none the richer for it.

In fact, if you were to return to that same piece of soil the following spring, you'd find "negative growth" still lying there where the bureaucrat left it, in a state of almost perfect preservation, except for minute parts of it that are slowly seeping down into the water table where they will eventually contaminate whole sections of the vernacular.

But enough of metaphors.

When visiting regions outside of your neighbourhood, you often must rely on printed words and symbols to help you distinguish good from evil. But signs do more than merely offer the traveller a map of local morality. They also reflect the attitude and state of mind of the people who made them. Interpreted together, they present a vivid sociological portrait – assuming you're in the mood for that sort of thing in the middle of a holiday.

While on a recent tour through several regions of Ontario, I dutifully recorded a number of the signs I saw. The ones I was most interested in were scrawled in an obviously unprofessional hand.

Here, then, are some of the folk laws of Ontario.

* * *

NOT TO BE USED AS A HAIRDRYER.

(Sign above a hand-dryer in a restroom in Tobermory, Ont.)

I don't know about you, but it would never have occurred to me to use one of these exasperating, supposedly hygienic tissue-substitutes to blow-dry my hair. I find it hard to muster the enthusiasm to use those blowers on my hands, let alone my head.

I bet no one has actually used a hand-blower on their hair. I bet it's just a fear that transfixed the owner of this particular Tobermory establishment one night in the middle of a nightmare.

This kind of sign is a pre-emptive sign. A possible variation on it is: "Not to be used as a nuclear weapon".

NO PERSONNEL CHEQUES OR CREDIT

(Sign in a dining lounge outside Sheguiandah, Ont.)

If you read this sign literally, what it means is that the employees of the dining lounge are not allowed to use cheques or credit, whereas members of the general public are free to pay for their meal with Canadian Tire money if they feel like it.

Perhaps this is not what was intended by the sign.

NO SMOKING, NO DRINKING, NO EATING,
NO FLOCKIN' AROUND.

(Sign in Green Acres Campsite store, Sheguiandah, Ont.)

After reading that sign I wished like hell there was a hand-blower in the store I could use as a hairdryer, since the sign neglected to include that crime.

Besides, there was no one to flock with in that store.

CAUTION. DO NOT ENTER

(Sign on a door leading outside at the top of a 111-year old lighthouse on the western tip of Manitoulin Island.)

This sign raised a philosophical question about the true nature of "in" and "out". Was it indeed possible, as the sign implied, to enter the outdoors?

The question left me so dizzy that I didn't dare step through the door to find out for myself.

PLEASE DO NOT SOIL GARMENTS

(Sign in a Tobermory gift shop)

This pleasant sign makes tourists feel as if they fell face-first into a cattle pasture, then rushed immediately over to the store to wipe their hands on a piece of clothing. (The owners of the store should consider installing hand-blowers.)

NO LOITERING OR DRINKING
IN FRONT OF THIS "BUILDING"

(Sign outside the Recreation Centre in Marathon, Ont.)

It's a good thing I spotted the sign. My wife and I were just about to saunter over to the front of the Recreation Centre and crack open a bottle of Cold Duck.

GRANNY'S KITCHEON

(Electric sign above a restaurant in downtown Marathon.)

The first thing I did upon arriving home from the vacation was to run to my *Oxford English Dictionary* to see if the word "kitchen" was spelled "kitcheon" in the distant past. It wasn't.

VEGETABLE FOR SALE

(Roadside sign near Blind River, Ont.)

I ask you: Is it worth pulling over for a single wax bean?

I - - - - ED MRS. LALONDE HERE

(Sign on a restroom door in Pancake Bay Provincial Park, on Lake Superior.)

The poignant aspect of this otherwise unremarkable piece of graffiti was that its writer obviously still respected "Mrs. Lalonde" after his discreet encounter with her. The polite reference to the lady, even in this vulgar context, somehow redeems the spirit of the whole message – particularly if it was written by Mr. Lalonde.

SMEDLEY WAS HERE

(Sign painted on a rock outcrop on Highway 17, north of Pancake Bay.)

At the edge of Lake Superior, you can look at Indian pictographs that are centuries old. Closer to the Trans-Canada Highway, more recent travellers have fashioned crude pictographs of their own. Most of them have nothing to do with art. In fact, usually all the viewer gets is a signature.

I chose this particular one because I get a kick out of picturing someone named Smedley scaling a chunk of billion-year-old granite merely to scratch out his name.

PLEASE DO NOT OPEN NEW MILK
UNTIL OLD ONE ALL GONE

(A message to all employees from Marino, manager of the Wayfarer Restaurant on the road to Nipigon, Ont.)

Every home should have a copy of this sign hanging in it. Marino, without knowing it, has given us a whole philosophy of life.

GENUINE FOOD
(Sign outside a restaurant near Gravenhurst, Ont.)
I bet this means hot beef sandwiches, as opposed to Creole Swordfish Almandine.

OUR WASHROOM FACILITIES ARE NOW RESERVED FOR OUR CAFE PATRONS ONLY DUE TO SEPTIC CAPABILITIES AND EXTREME CUSTOMER ABUSE ...
HAVE A PLEASANT DAY
(Sign on the front of a store in Campbellville, Ont.)
A salutation prefaced by a plumbing lecture – what a great gimmick to bring in new business!

NO IN & OUT PRIVILEGES.
(Sign in a parking lot on Church St. in Toronto, Ont.)
Fair enough: All I want to do is park the car.

HORESES BOARDED.
(Roadside sign on Highway 6, Flamborough, Ont.)
If I had a horese – whatever that is – I promise I would board it there.

NO SMOKING. NO SWEARING. PUT ALL GARBAGE IN PAIL.
NO BANGING MACHINES. LIMIT OF ONE CREDIT PER PERSON.
LET OTHERS HAVE A TURN. NO EATING WHAT-SO-EVER.
FOLLOW THE RULES OR LEAVE. THANK-YOU. THE MANAGEMENT.
(Sign above pinball machines in a variety store in Hamilton, Ont.)
Why do I imagine this sign etched on a stone tablet on Mount Sinai?

DANCING LADIES
(Sign outside a restaurant-tavern in Caledon, Ont.)
Naked ladies might have been a little more to the point.

WE WELCOME WELL-BEHAVED CHILDREN.
(Sign in the entrance to a restaurant in Ancaster, Ont.)
Are we to infer that the establishment doesn't welcome well-behaved adults?

JOE KAPPOTTO IS ALIVE AND WELL AND LIVING IN KENILWORTH.
(Graffito in a restaurant washroom, Elora, Ont.)
I just thought I'd pass the word on to Joe's friends and relatives and creditors.

LIMITED EDITION PRINTS ON WOOD FASHIONED AFTER THE PRIMATIVE STYLE.
(Sign in arts and crafts store, Campbellville.)
But why the "primative" spelling? Could this perhaps be folk-orthography?

THE REAL THINGS OF LIFE ARE SO OBVIOUS,
PEOPLE HAVE TO SAY THERE'S MORE TO IT
THAN MEETS THE EYE.
(Graffito in restaurant washroom, Toronto, Ont.)
Tell that to Joe Kappotto, who announces his existence on washroom walls.

(August 5, 1987)

USE ONLY AS DIRECTED

A week ago last Thursday, I learned that I have been washing my hair for the past several months with an anti-acne treatment.

Like virtually every other human being on earth, I had my share of acne during adolescence. But I don't recall the problem ever spreading to my scalp. In short, my inadvertent efforts to stop acne before it starts have been for nought, with untold environmental consequences for what's left of my hair.

Where I went wrong, my daughter informed me, was in concluding that just because the plastic bottle containing the anti-acne treatment had the word "shampoo" on it meant that this was an advisable substance to use on my hair.

For years I have been trying to negotiate a Shampoo And Conditioner Non-Proliferation Treaty with my family. Our shower resembles a missile silo, right down to the menacing cluster of cosmetic warheads. We possess a dizzying array of pump-action, squeeze-action and pour-action containers that dispense fluids for the multiple hair-affliction scenarios of modern life: split ends, lack of body, oiliness, dryness, the dreaded frizzies,chemically treated hair, normal hair – you name the problem, we own the solution.

Having grown up on a single brand of shampoo, which I dutifully purchased on the strength of its advertisements about dandruff and related public-service messages concerning the heartbreak of psoriasis, I have always considered the current specialized approach more of an ingenious marketing tactic than a genuine strategic breakthrough in the war against bad hair.

Faced with our family's arsenal of chemical weapons in the shower, I have had no choice but to become conversant in the technology behind them. That's why it's all the more galling to learn I've been fighting non-existing acne in lieu of washing my hair for the past few months. (The stuff is primarily meant to be applied to one's face, I now understand.)

What with the cornucopia of cosmetic agents at my disposal, it's a wonder I haven't done any visibly permanent damage to myself. A cursory inventory of the hair products alone in my bathroom reads like a list of gizmos from a science-fiction novel:

* Sculpting Lotion Intercellular Extension
* Fast-Drying Super-Hold Styling Spray
* Permanent Wave Rejuvenator
* Phylogenic/Botanical Deep-Penetrating Hair Reconstructor & Ultra Hold Spray
* Leave-on Conditioner Treatment

Rampant specialization has been the trend throughout the cosmetics industry in recent years. For instance, you almost have to take a night course to keep up with the changes in tanning-lotion technology in recent years. Whereas in the good old days you simply bought a bottle of tanning lotion and rubbed it on your skin to prevent sunburn, nowadays you have a seemingly infinite variety of sunscreen gradients from which to choose.

Should you choose too strong a sunscreen, you might stay as pale as Wonder Bread despite two weeks of systematic sunbathing. Should you purchase a weak sunscreen, you could turn into a lobster in a matter of minutes.

The ideal strategy, from the cosmetic industry's point of view, is to buy a bottle of each of the various susncreens and to graduate slowly from one bottle to the next, with a bank loan to show for your trouble.

* * *

Increased awareness of the carcinogenic effects of sunbathing is usually cited as the reason for the complex line of tanning agents available to the buying public. But I can't shake the suspicion that it's a question of providing the consumer with a forest of choices in the hope that individual trees will go unseen.

Cold remedies have undergone the same specialization revolution. You must choose among "non-drowsy" cold remedies for dry, hacking coughs (the "non-drowsy" ingredient is usually caffeine), "drowsy" cold remedies for phlegmy coughs that can be ingested as long as you don't operate heavy machinery after taking as directed, and hot lemon drinks that relieve more symptoms than you ever imagined you could possibly have at one time.

Considering the sheer complexity of therapeutic options available to them, it's a wonder people bother to get sick anymore.

(February 25, 1990)

THE OFF-COLOUR COMMENTATOR

I went to a Blue Jay game a few weeks ago. We had good seats behind home plate. The game was exciting. A young man sitting directly behind me screamed the "F" word an average of 12 times per inning, if you take into account the fact that the Jays didn't come to bat in the ninth.

I'm no stranger to swearing. I have been known to utter the "F" word on rare occasions, for dramatic emphasis. But to this young man it was Basic English. I marvelled as he ran it through all its possible applications – verb, noun, adjective, pronoun, prefix, suffix.

Not once, I remember noting, did the young man use the "F" word to convey the meaning it is most usually understood to convey. I found this interesting.

At some point I would have liked to settle into the ball game and forget about the young man and his "F" word. But he was intoxicated and the liquor lent a vivid, sandpapery edge to his baritone voice. When he yelled the "F" word to a Chicago White Sox batter by the name of Greg Luzinski, most of the players on the field – especially Mr. Luzinski, who is not a small man – glared into the stands behind home plate.

I got the impression Mr. Luzinski thought I was the man who was screaming. I went for a hot dog to prove otherwise.

I could still hear the young man from the hot dog stand.

"Who is that guy anyway?" said the girl serving me the hot dog.

"He sits behind me, behind home plate," I told her.

"He's gross," the girl said.

"I don't know him," I said.

As I ate my foot-long and watched the Jays try to protect a late-inning one-run lead, my fascination with the swearer and his swearing did not abate. What is it about certain words, I asked myself, that makes them taboo, and consequently so attractive to a fellow such as the one behind me?

"Luzinski, you big - - - -," the swearer bellowed. Again, Mr. Luzinski glared up into the stands. I pointed to my hot dog, to the fact that my mouth was full.

What if we all decided one day that the "F" word was perfectly OK, I wondered. What if it were decreed that it and all the other swear words were acceptable any place and anytime? Would no one say them anymore, ever again? Or would the young man behind me invent a whole new set of words to replace them?

For that matter, what do swear words do? What are they for? Could it be that if this guy weren't swearing to beat the band, he'd be letting off steam in a more physically destructive way? Maybe words like the "F" word are necessary safety valves so people like this young man can give vent to their frustrations without doing any lasting harm.

I decided perhaps all he needed was a little understanding. I turned in my seat to face him.

"Excuse me. I couldn't help but notice–"

He stood up. So did everybody else. A White Sox player was rounding third; it was going to be a close play at home. "Mow him down, you - - - - er," the young man screamed, his left arm flailing the air. The flailing arm clipped my cup of rancid coffee and spilled it onto the jacket on the seat to my right. I quickly bent down to lift the jacket before the coffee seeped into the fabric. So did the woman next to me who owned the jacket. Our heads knocked together.

We were both still in a daze as the crowd around us rejoiced at the close play which ended up being the third out, which ended up being the end of the game. Neither of us had seen it.

"I'm sorry," I said to the woman. "I was just–"

"Are you crazy or something?" the woman said.

I shook my head. The crowd was filing out of the stands. The young man I'd been trying to help was long gone.

"Jeepers," I said to myself. The word didn't relieve me at all.

(June 13, 1984)

IF MARIGOLDS COULD SPEAK

Not far from where you would turn off the Gardiner Expressway to visit Ontario Place if you were westbound and the weather were not freezing drizzle, the botanical ads on the right-hand slope catch your eye. (The fact that you are cruising at nine miles per hour helps your eye to be caught.)

You're not sure who invented the concept of botanical advertising, but you would like to commission the forging of a large, heavy medal to honour this person, and you would personally like to pin said medal to the skin of said person's chest.

You've seen the ads, made of live vegetable matter on a bed of what looks like landscaping gravel, countless times on your trips to and from newspaper assignments in Toronto. But you've trained your mind to blot out the various brand names these miserable plants have been trained to spell out.

(Actually, you remember one name, Minolta, because you've always thought Minolta would be a pretty name for a mermaid, or for the goddess of fashion photographers – not that you've ever personally owned a Minolta.)

You wonder if somewhere in the vast trackless regions of Ontario bushland to the north and west of where you currently are, some enterprising logging company has sculpted the brand name of a beer to inspire the thirst of bush pilots plying the unfettered skies of God's country.

It would take maybe a half-mile of carefully managed birch forest to spell out "Ex Says It All".

* * *

You have seen topiary displays of shrubs carefully sculpted to represent wild animals and other shapes one doesn't normally associate with shrubs. You have read Stephen King's novel, *The Shining*, in which the topiary garden on the grounds of the Overlook Hotel comes to life and menaces a maniac and his family.

You have seen flowers used to bold and lovely effect in front of municipal buildings across the land, and to gaudy and American effect in Pasadena's Rose Bowl Parade. You have asked yourself if roses would be more impressive blooming in the soil than gracing a mammoth float of impish Smurfs who wave cheerfully to the kids and little old ladies from Pasadena, not to mention a television audience of millions.

You have crusaded in print on behalf of the lowly dandelion, fair flower of springtime, which has been consigned to the ash heap of garden culture despite its lovely yellow appearance, its musky bouquet, the sublime fluff of its seed and the fact that passable wine can be made from the leaves.

But you have never felt as strongly about the fate of a few plants as you do about the way these particular plants you're gazing at from the Gardiner Expressway in the late afternoon rush hour have been enslaved by humans to serve a purely mercantile role.

* * *

Thank goodness yours is a culture of short attention spans and instant gratification. Otherwise you'd likely see miles of Boston ivy spreading across the billboards of the land, painstakingly trained by their human masters to spell out slogans and brand names. Thank goodness Boston ivy dares to spread at such a leisurely rate.

You've always had an instinctive affinity for English gardens, because the tendency in them is to let the plants and flowers find a semblance of natural disorder for themselves. An English garden is the horticultural antonym of a French garden where crocuses, pansies, daffodils and petunias are conditioned from birth to grow in geometric lines and to keep off the grass.

Nowadays at Versailles, in a little village of thatched huts Marie Antoinette ordered built so that she and her aristocrat chums could play peasant, the front yard of one of the huts glows a blinding yellow in the summertime with a non-geometrical profusion of marigolds. These marigolds appear to have taken the French revolution to heart: No more Mr. Nice Plant.

A couple of hundred yards from where the marigolds are asserting liberty, equality and sorority, endless parallel lines of stately trees adorn the backyard of the house Louis XIV built. Classical statuary stand at equidistant points relative to the ranks of trees. A gigantic bronze Neptune rises out of an ornamental pool. The impression, thoroughly intended, is one of total human domination over nature.

As the traffic edges sluggishly ahead on the Gardiner Expressway, you wish one of those botanical ads on the right-hand slope would discover graffiti and grow itself into a four-letter word.

(February 4, 1989)

HOW TO ACCUMULATE BOOKS

It was several years ago that we began to receive urgent-looking notifications from the people in the Sweepstakes Department of *Reader's Digest*. What all these notifications had in common was the fairly emphatic implication that we were about to become rich beyond our wildest dreams.

Since then, the urgent-looking notifications have continued to arrive by post on a regular basis, but the only material riches we have now that we didn't have then are a pile of *Reader's Digest* books my wife has been kind enough to order while filling out and returning the endless series of Sweepstakes forms.

Our home library has expanded to include such irreplaceable large-format hardcover volumes as *Household Hints & Handy Tips, The Practical Problem Solver, Illustrated Reverse Dictionary, ABC's Of The Human Body, Great Disasters (Dramatic True Stories Of Nature's Awesome Powers), Guide To Gardening In Canada, Legal Question & Answer Book, Action Guide: What To Do In An Emergency*, and last but certainly not least, *How To Do Just About Anything*.

Among other things, the latter book shows me in clear and concise detail how to make mayonnaise, control mealybugs, open stuck jar lids, treat frostbite, make French-fried potatoes, prune trees, stay afloat vertically in water, silence noisy footwear, build a lean-to, cure diarrhea, walk with a crutch, cope with minor coughs, mend china, adjust a carburetor, train a bonsai tree and give up smoking.

The recent arrival of *How To Do Just About Anything* drove home to me the seriousness of my wife's apparent addiction to *Reader's Digest* self-help books. Obviously she had decided that our copies of *Practical Problem Solver* and *Household Hints & Handy Tips* didn't adequately protect us from the various practical dilemmas of daily life.

My wife is prepared to admit she may be suffering from a rare book-acquiring disorder that is not covered in any of the *Reader's Digest* volumes we have so far received. When I pointed out to her that *Practical Problem Solver* suggested, among other things, that an overturned frisbee could be used as a cookie tray at a child's birthday party, she was willing to agree that perhaps this was not absolutely essential knowledge.

But she nevertheless felt compelled to argue that the same book had quite valuably advised us to carry worms in a can of moist coffee grounds, since the coffee grounds make it easier to take the worms out of the can while fishing.

"We don't fish," I said.

"We may fish at some point," she replied, still far from cured.

I don't dare show my wife the page in *Household Hints & Handy Tips* that advises readers to "show off your special treasures in a brilliant display case; install mirrors all around a wall niche and fit it with glass shelves." So far, her voluminous collection of *Reader's Digest* books is discreetly tucked away next to genuine, actual reference books.

I am, however, tempted to leave *Household Hints & Handy Tips* lying conspicuously in the living room, open to the page that states: "Eliminating clutter cuts down on the need to clean things, because an uncluttered home, even though not spotless, looks better than one that is dust-free but strewn with odds and ends."

In the meantime, I'm pleased to see that my wife has not yet placed an order for *Great Battles Of WWII*, which was enclosed with the latest urgent-looking notification from the Sweepstakes Department.

Her reluctance to order *Great Battles Of WWII* might stem from the fact that there is more than enough violence and mayhem for her to peruse in *Action Guide: What To Do In An Emergency*. That book devotes entire pages to such worst-case scenarios as When A Crowd Turns Ugly, Escaping From A Volcanic Eruption and What To Do If A Bomb Goes Off.

Oddly enough, there's no mention anywhere of what to do when your collection of *Reader's Digest* books becomes a fire hazard.

(February 16, 1991)

2.

THE NUMBERS OF ALL OUR DAYS

I AM NOT EUCLID

Scientists at Chevron Geosciences Co., in Los Angeles, were trying out the oil company's new "super computer" when it happened to spit out the largest prime number known up to now. Space and time prevent me from passing this number on to you. It contains 65,060 digits.

Big numbers, of themselves, are not all that remarkable. What's perhaps most remarkable about big numbers is that they continue to infinity. In other words, there is no such thing as the biggest number – or the smallest fraction, for that matter.

Prime numbers are a somewhat more intricate affair, since they must be divisible only by themselves and the number 1. Four, for example, is not a prime number because it can be divided by 2. Turning up a 65,060-digit number that can be divided only by itself and 1 is probably cause to go out for a beer.

Since around 300 B.C., mathematicians have been studying prime numbers. Two of the earliest mathematicians, Euclid and Eratosthenes, accomplished quite a bit without computers. And perhaps the most significant breakthrough in prime-number lore occurred around the turn of the century, when kids were still counting on their fingers.

According to my research, conclusive proof was found around this time that "as the natural number *n* becomes greater and greater, the number of prime numbers less than or equal to *n* tends to the quotient of number *n* divided by the natural logarithm of *n*."

It's a pity I can't understand what this breakthrough means. If I did, I would pass it on to you. In fact, one of the greatest regrets of my life is that I am useless at mathematics. After 13 years of formal education in this discipline, all I can do is add, subtract, multiply and divide.

My Grade 13 math teacher didn't care for me, primarily because I regularly fell asleep in his class. I don't mean "asleep" in the figurative sense. I mean "asleep" in the sense that your muscles go slack and the sheep in your head start jumping the fence unbidden and uncounted.

No insult is intended to this undoubtedly gifted pedagogue, but he was unable to convince me that math, for its own sake, was a beautiful and rewarding discipline. Maybe it was the latent fascism of the subject that put me off when I was young – the idea that numbers unquestioningly obey laws.

On an examination question in just about all the other subjects, I found that I was able to give shading and tone to my answer by embellishing the main theme with graceful, extended passages of gibberish.

In math, if I was calculating the square root of 312 and got the first step of my answer wrong, I was doomed to be wrong the rest of the way. This struck me as arbitrary and vexatious, leaving no room for the full flowering of human creativity, i.e. the art of sounding like you know what you're talking about.

As a consequence, my mathematics mark at the end of my second term in Grade 13 was 5 per cent. This prime number wreaked havoc with my general academic average and raised the very real doubt that I would be able to do well enough in the final term to pull off a passing grade.

To minimize the embarrassment both to myself and my math teacher, I attended very few of the math classes in my final term. In fact, I did not attend a single class. But such are the vicissitudes of Bell curves and other political-academic considerations that I ended up with a final mark of 17 per cent.

When I encountered my math teacher on the last day of school, I told him I planned to study fine arts in University. He said this was a wise move on my part. Left totally unacknowledged was the fact that my math mark had risen more than 200 per cent in the final term, from 5 to 17. This was by far the single most dramatic improvement in the entire class.

Since I had achieved such a stunning reversal in my academic fortunes without attending one class, I tried to calculate what my final mark might have been had I not attended my math class all that year, instead of just the final term.

But that's an algebra problem. I don't remember algebra.

(September 25, 1985)

MANY UNHAPPY RETURNS

It has become a solemn tradition in our house to fill out our income tax forms on April 29 and mail them on April 30. This way the Federal Government does not reap any extra interest from the money we invariably owe it.

In taxation matters, it's customary for my wife to do the filling out and for me to do the mailing, chiefly because I don't know how to do the filling out.

My wife adds a little drama to the ritual every year by misplacing one or more pertinent documents. Last year, she misplaced my T-4 slip. This year, she misplaced her T-4 slip and my entire tax return form. Next year, her tax return form, my T-4 slip and several blocks of southwest Hamilton will probably slip into another dimension of time and space.

Because of the misplaced documents, we were unable to fill out our tax returns on April 29 this year. I had no choice but to drive to the downtown post office late the following evening and personally drop off the forms so they would bear the all-important April 30 postmark.

"Oh great," I said. "Now all of Hamilton will know how stupid we are to wait to the last minute."

"Don't worry," said my wife. "Nobody's downtown after dark on a Wednesday."

* * *

The traffic cop trying to sort out the tremendous traffic jam downtown the following evening showed considerable grace under pressure.

"Why don't some of you idiots do your income tax on the 29th?"

"I do, I do," I protested. "My wife misplaced a few documents," I began to tell him when the car ahead of me lurched forward and I had no choice but to lurch after it.

After finding a parking space near Jackson Square, I tried to blend in with the throng marching eastward to the post office. Telltale grey envelopes in hand, we were like biblical Israelites trudging out of the wilderness and into the frying pan.

"I wouldn't have to be doing this if my wife hadn't misplaced a few documents," I explained to the man trudging next to me.

"Women!" he snorted. "You can't fill out your income tax return with them, you can't fill out your income tax return without them."

The traffic cop recognized me at the door of the post office. "You again," he said. "You're the idiot with the wife who–"

"–misplaced a few documents," I said. "Could you keep your voice down?"

* * *

The first man to greet me inside the post office was the mayor, who stood by the door. He was shaking the hand of everyone who passed him. Not far from the mayor, a man sold candied apples from a trolley. Further away, by the stamp counter, a brass band performed selections from popular Broadway musicals of bygone years.

WELCOME PROCRASTINATORS, said a large banner hanging from the ceiling. A young woman handed colourful helium balloons to the children. The brass band lit into "Tomorrow". I swallowed my self-esteem and sauntered in the direction of the brass band. I needed stamps.

Before the man at the stamp counter could open his mouth, I said to him: " I am not a procrastinator. It's a tradition in our house to fill out our income tax returns on April 29. Unfortunately my wife misplaced a few documents yesterday, which forced us to–"

"At last!" a man in a loud sports jacket said as he grabbed me by the elbow. The sudden glare of TV lights and camera flashbulbs blinded me. "Congratulations! You are the 10,000th Hamilton taxpayer to wait foolishly until the last day to mail his income tax form at the central post office! Are there any thoughts you'd like to share with us?"

"My wife misplaced a few documents," I said. "Could you keep your voice down?"

Too late. The mayor, ever sensitive to the presence of TV lights and camera flashes, almost crushed my hand as he congratulated me with his booming voice and gummy grin. Children with buttons that said IT'S A WONDER THEY EVER GOT AROUND TO CONCEIVING ME cheered wildly. The brass band played the theme from *Same Time Next Year* in my honour.

Later, the man in the loud sports jacket handed me a slip of paper with an address where I could pick up my prize the next day. I could tell by the look on his face that he knew I'd never get around to picking the prize up--or that my wife would misplace the slip of paper.

(May 7, 1986)

DON'T TAKE ANY STYROFOAM NICKELS

One of the most vivid dreams I had as a child was of going to the schoolyard with a shovel and digging up piles of money. All those people who comb beaches and parks in the summertime with their metal detectors probably had the same dream when they were young.

In my dream, it wasn't bills I turned up with the shovel, just a limitless number of coins with which to feed pop and pinball machines for the rest of my life. Like all children and metal detectors, I knew coins were where it was at. Coins were money you had fun with. Paper bills, on the other hand, were what you were given for being grown up, to pay debts.

Coins have been around for so much of human history that their allure is embedded in our genes. Folding money is a much more recent aberration, like those infernal cheques with the scenic pictures on them. Does anyone actually find it easier to part with their wealth on a cheque with a scenic picture?

So it is without sadness or regret that I greet the news that the Royal Canadian Mint is phasing out the $1 bill in favour of a coin roughly the size of a quarter.

The mint will have to decide between a gold-plated coin and a cheaper, brass-plated coin. Either is preferable to paper. Check the nearest available chart of anniversary symbols. Paper ranks the lowest, representing one year – only somewhat better than uranium (six months) and PCBs (five minutes).

In Britain, the recent introduction of a 1-pound coin met with a lot of specious opposition. One Tory MP referred to it as "a horrid little button". But what is a 1-pound note made of? The same material you blow your nose with. Better a button than a kleenex, I say.

There are at least five hundred things wrong with paper money. I won't get into all of them, but:

* if you are especially wealthy, you are a walking fire hazard.
* when you drop a coin, it usually alerts you to the situation by clanging when it hits the ground. When you drop paper money, it flutters soundlessly, conspiratorially to earth, where it waits for a complete stranger to find it and spend it on your behalf.

* Paper is an excellent germ-carrier. When it changes hands, so do millions of viruses (and since we all have this secret habit at one time or another of smelling our dollar bills, the viruses get into our lungs and wreak havoc from there).
* Imagine you're a scuba-diver who has discovered a sunken chest from a 200-year-old pirate ship. Imagine the chest contains nothing but paper money. Imagine your disappointment when you confront all that useless sludge.
* Many persons snort dangerous drugs with paper money. Try snorting anything with a coin.
* When was the last time a coin of yours got torn, or ripped in two?
* When was the last time you had to iron a coin before a change machine would accept it and spit out smaller denominations?
* If you have a piggy bank and you want to shake it to see how much money you have, you don't hear a thing if it's full of paper money.
* It doesn't stack neatly on a poker table.
* It's made of dead trees.
* You can't open the battery compartment of your camera with it.
* If you are unable to make up your mind about something, try flipping a dollar bill to decide.
* When was the last time you saw paper money in a wishing well?
* Try getting the tone-arm of an old hi-fi record player to work properly by scotch-taping a dollar bill onto it.

Since we live at a time when a small piece of plastic represents liquid sums of money we don't even possess, a shift back to a more substantial form of currency is overdue. Ideally, a coin should represent its own exact value in terms of the substance it's made of (let's avoid styrofoam, if possible).

Years ago, when paper currency was introduced, a tentative answer was provided to the question, "Do you think money grows on trees?" Now that the point has been made, let us re-embrace coins with zeal. Let us fortify the stitching of our pockets and purses, and not spend it all in one place.

(November 21, 1984)

TRAGEDY OF A VERY DIM BULB

All he wanted was a couple of 60-watt lightbulbs. He went to the small hardware store around the corner, picked up a package containing a couple of 60-watt bulbs and set it down on the cashier's counter.

"We have a special on another brand of bulbs," the cashier said. "You get four bulbs at a reduced price, plus you get a free camera."

"A free camera?" he said.

The cashier came out from behind the counter, went to the lightbulb display and showed him the brand that was on special. Sure enough, there were four bulbs in the package, as well as a small camera that already had film in it.

He had not been in the market for a camera that afternoon, but he found it hard to resist the idea of getting one for free, so he bought the special reduced package of bulbs.

That was his first mistake.

* * *

Within a week or so of purchasing the lightbulbs, he actually got around to deploying them in the house.

"Let's see that free camera you were talking about," his wife said. He fished in the cupboard under the sink among numerous empty cans and bottles of cleaning agents and extricated the two remaining bulbs and the free camera. The brand name of the camera was *Love*.

The little yellow box the camera came in stated that the camera was "fully loaded with colour film to give you 20 exposures and 60 colour prints." There didn't appear to be any instructions inside the box – just a sickly little black disposable camera.

"It's a sickly little black disposable camera and there aren't any instructions," he told his wife. On the back of the camera was the inscription "Fabricado por sonora industrial zona france de mansaus. MADE IN BRAZIL. Parente registrada."

He wondered what the Spanish words meant. Maybe it was a disclaimer of some kind that he should know about.

"Bring the camera here and take a picture of the cat," his wife said. "She's wrestling with the throw rug again."

He threw the little yellow box into the garbage, rushed into the living room and snapped a half-dozen pictures of the cat wrestling with the throw rug. It only occurred to him afterward that the camera did not have a built-in flash.

"Isn't that thing supposed to have a flash?" his wife inquired.

He took the camera back to the hardware store and asked one of the clerks what sort of flashbulb went with it. The young clerk examined the camera, then led him the flashbulb display, picked a package of flashcubes dangling from a long metal hook, handed it to him and said "This should do the trick, I think."

He paid for the flashcubes and rushed home to take more pictures of the cat, but by then the cat was fast asleep on top of the piano.

"Great," he sighed. "What do I take pictures of now?"

"Why don't you wait until the cat wakes up?" said his wife.

"I don't want to wait until the cat wakes up," he said. " I want to try these flashcubes now."

He fired off three or four pictures of his wife seated on the sofa, glaring up at him. A couple of times the flash more or less flashed.

* * *

On the yellow box which had contained the camera was an address to which he was supposed to send the camera to have the film processed at no charge. By the time he realized this, the yellow box was deep in the garbage, under eggshells, cigarette ashes and coffee grounds. He had no choice but to go to the hardware store and jot down the address from another yellow box.

He rattled the door of the hardware store a few times. The young clerk materialized from somewhere and mouthed the words "We're closed."

He explained that all he wanted was to copy an address from one of the boxes.

"Come back on Monday," the clerk said.

"I can't wait until Monday," he heard himself reply.

The clerk sighed and unlocked the door.

* * *

A couple of weeks later, the manila envelope containing his camera came back with INSUFFICIENT POSTAGE stamped on it.

"I told you two stamps wouldn't be enough postage," his wife said helpfully.

To avoid repeating the mistake, he drove downtown to the central post office, parked his car outside the door, dashed in, had the package weighed, paid the extra postage and dashed out. By then, the man from the parking authority was two-thirds through writing a parking ticket.

"I'm here, I'm here, I'm here," he said to the man from the parking authority.

"So's this," said the man, handing him the ticket.

"I was here no more than 45 seconds," he protested.

"Tell it to a judge," the man from the parking authority replied and walked off.

The judge said he was moved by the defence counsel's eloquent account of his client's fragile emotional state the day he briefly parked his car in front of the post office. But, said the judge, the law must be seen to be upheld.

He paid the parking fine on his way out of court. His lawyer said he would send his bill in the mail.

The day the bill arrived, he sat down at his desk to study the itemized list of expenses that totalled $289. He got out his pen and added that figure to the parking fine, the postage, the flashcubes, miscellaneous expenses and the intangible mental and emotional strain involving in receiving the free camera. Late afternoon merged with early evening and still he hunched over the figures and receipts.

He switched on his desk lamp. It didn't work. He called down to his wife to bring him one of the four bulbs he had purchased for a total of $347.34.

"I've already put one of those new bulbs in your lamp," his wife replied.

He tried the lamp again. The room was still dark.

(December 17, 1988)

A JUNKIE'S CONFESSION

After scanning old toasters, countless effigies of animals, assorted utensils and Red Rose Tea figurines at three locations over the course of four hours on a Sunday afternoon, the following question occurred to me: What do people see in flea markets, anyway?

The question is naive, of course. Flea markets are flourishing in this part of the world for at least two obvious reasons.

1. They successfully combine a couple of highly popular human pastimes -- shopping and poking around other people's junk.
2. They are the only action in Ontario on a Sunday.

To tell the truth, I have often been mystified by the popularity of doughnut shops as well. It's been said if you set all the doughnuts eaten each year in the greater Hamilton-Burlington area side by side, the holes alone would stretch halfway around the globe.

Could there be some strange correlation between doughnut shops and flea markets -- some subconscious compartment of the mind in which these two seemingly separate enterprises prey on our weakness for cheap and/or fattening things?

I'm suprised no one has yet opened a store that sells doughnuts, strong coffee and second-hand utensils -- all under the same roof.

* * *

Lest readers suspect I am commenting from some ivory tower of consumer superiority, I should make it clear I am a chronic flea marketeer. (I'm no stranger to honey-dipped delights, either.)

In other words, I know how serious these afflictions can become. Here's a case history:

Because of flea markets, my wife has developed an abiding interest in Depression glass -- cheap, machine-made dishes that sold for pennies in the dirty 30's. Our house has become a kind of Depression-glass shrine. We now sip tea from green glass mugs that were popular in all the Kresge's stores in the 1950's. We eat our meals off smoke-grey glass plates that belong on the hubs of automobile wheels.

Last Sunday, my wife bought a set of powder-blue Depression-glass salt and pepper shakers. The gentleman who sold them noted they were large enough that you had to fill them with salt and pepper only once in a lifetime. That must be what convinced my wife to buy them; otherwise she would have been deterred by their sheer, consummate ugliness.

Our daughter, who stands one day to inherit the two shakers and the rest of this treasure trove of cheap, machine-made glass, has already made it clear she wants no part of the stuff. She says she prefers the more precious heirlooms her mother has packed away to make room for her latest acquisition: Depression-glass refrigerator dishes.

"Just look at them," my wife exulted. "They were around before plastic came along."

What she neglects to mention is *why* plastic came along.

* * *

In an era of almost instant obsolescence, junk is the opiate of the masses. Junk in mint condition is the most potent narcotic of all.

Take it from a junkie:

Who can accurately gauge the street value of a pristine copy of Lester Lanin's *High Society* LP? Obviously not the man at the Fergus flea market who sold it to me last Sunday for 50 cents.

Lester Lanin is a society band-leader who was briefly popular a quarter-century ago. His *High Society* LP consists of a medley of popular show tunes from the era. The reason I was so excited by this find is that Lester Lanin is peerless: He dares to go one step beyond mere Muzak into previously unexplored realms of banality.

Lester Lanin's orchestra arrangements are so repetitive that it was only after about an hour that I realized the needle was locked in the groove. Where else can you find this kind of mind-numbing distraction ... other than perhaps a doughnut shop?

This past summer in Hagar, Ontario, I happened upon an LP of bland standards by Bert Kaempfert And His Orchestra.

"How much," I asked the vendor.

"I'm firm at $2," the vendor said.

"I'll give you 50 cents," I said.

"It's a deal," he said.

We both came away happy.

(September 24, 1986)

THE ECONOMIC CLIMATE

It was the end of another long day. On my way home, I stopped into the corner store for bread and milk.

"Howdy," said the ever-friendly man behind the counter. "Quite a downturn out there."

"Pardon me?" I said.

"Downturn. Conference Board of Canada's medium-term outlook is for a near recession with continuing high unemployment and interest rates unless deficits are cut. I don't know about you, but I'm stocking up on investment certificates for the winter."

"Yes. Certificates," I said, having not the foggiest notion what he was talking about. A woman over by the chocolate bars perked up.

"My bank's forecasting a growth recession, Ed," she told the storekeeper. "Low inflation and sluggish growth. Might not be as bad as the Conference Board says."

"You can't believe a bank," Ed answered with a bit of a smirk. "They tell shareholders one thing and the public another. Isn't that so?" he said, looking at me.

"Well ... "

"Hi Ed," said a middle-aged man I recognized, who lived down the street. He was rubbing his hands together, as if trying to keep warm. "If I didn't know better, I'd swear we're in for a deep recession. I just looked at the economic indicators."

"I used to keep an old economic indicator in my window right here," Ed said to me. " I liked to watch the mercury rise and fall, but it discouraged the customers so I have it hanging in the stockroom window now, to remind the hired help that these are tough times."

"That's nice," I said.

"You can't trust economic indicators anymore, Ed," said the woman by the chocolate bars. "The economy's so unpredictable this time of year you never know what investment portfolio to wear from one day to the next."

"Too true," said the middle-aged man, shaking his head.

In walked one of the elder statesmen of the neighbourhood. "You better insulate your storefront, Ed," he announced. "Looks like we're in for a deceleration. I can feel it in my joints."

"That's what the OECD forecasts," a scruffy young man piped in from over by the video games.

"Mind your mouth," Ed snapped at him.

"The kid's right about the OECD," said the postman, who had finished his route and was in for his customary pint of chocolate milk. "They figure the GDP is going to fall like cats and dogs."

"See?" said the boy.

The barber who owns the shop next door stepped in. "Hi Ed. Enough stagflation for ya?"

"You're joking," said the woman by the chocolate bars.

"That's what StatsCan forecasts," the barber shrugged. "Not much movement now through next year."

"The Canadian Chamber of Commerce still predicts we're gonna have prolonged growth," said a police officer, just in from his day on the foot beat.

"Yeah, but will the growth be malignant or benign – that's the question," said the middle-aged man, nudging me in the ribs.

"What about this rebound I've been hearing about?" Ed said.

"You mean the Economic Council of Canada forecast," said the policeman. "You've got to remember, Ed, that the Ontario Economic Council said people with fixities will still be looking for protection from the public sector, no matter what."

"You've got a point there," said Ed.

"Anyway," said the boy at the video game, " the OECD says the manufacturing sector failed to pay enough attention to competitiveness and now it faces a big adjustment."

"Who asked you?" said the policeman. "Is he bothering you, Ed?"

"Naw," said Ed. "He's only a smart aleck."

The woman plunked a chocolate bar down on the counter. "Just the other day, one of the experts at Montreal Trust said all the debate about how to fight the deficit was more gratuitous comment than meaningful analysis."

"You can say that again," said the postman.

"Just the other day ..." the woman in the store began saying again when I fled the store.

"What took you so long," my wife wanted to know. I told her I had been chatting with a few of the neighbours.

"What about?"

"The weather," I said.

(October 24, 1984)

3.

UNDERSTANDING MEDIA

YOU BORN TODAY

On Monday of this week, my *Spectator* horoscope advised me to "take special care in handling sharp objects." This advice struck me as scarcely more astrological than the time-honoured injunction to look both ways before crossing the street.

The only logical reason the warning about sharp objects could have been in my horoscope that day was that Sydney Omarr and his team of researchers had discovered from their various computations that people born under Gemini are in above-average danger from sharp objects.

Why, in that case, didn't Sydney and his fellow horoscopers simply advise all Geminis to stay away from sharp objects altogether? Besides, I look to the daily horoscope for up-to-the-minute reports on potential domestic adjustments and career opportunities, not for an unusually blunt warning that sounds like I'm about to stumble into the business end of an scimitar.

The fact that I consulted my horoscope a scant few minutes after getting an unusually nasty paper-cut from the self-same section of the self-same *Spectator* gave me a sneaky feeling Sydney Omarr and his people had it in for me. Then again, the Monday horoscope is supposed to apply to what happens to you on Tuesday, so they were more or less off the hook.

* * *

Most of us are familiar with the rudiments of astrology, a science-of-sorts that places us under one of 12 signs of the zodiac according to our date of birth and other pertinent facts. Most of us have formed an opinion of one kind or another about astrology in general and Sydney Omarr's brand of astrology in particular.

It seems many of us are more willing to accept the validity of the various personality-traits ascribed to the 12 signs of the Zodiac than the idea that an astrologer can divine that "while looking for something else you locate the missing cash," as Sydney Omarr's message to Aries people informed them last Monday.

If any persons living under the sign of Aries located some cash while looking for something else on or about Sept. 18, 1990, I would like to hear from them.

Usually, the daily newspaper horoscopists sidestep the need to actually see into the future by couching their daily blurbs in deliberately non-specific language such as "focus on essentials" (Leo) and "avoid driving with one who is bibulous" (Virgo).

Why then, were all Geminis warned about interfacing with something as specific as a sharp object on Tuesday?

* * *

It's surprising that astrologers have had a monopoly on the mumbo-jumbo component of newspapers for so long. It's surprising that mentalists, oracles and readers of sheep entrails haven't occasionally been approached by some papers as potential alternatives to the fuzzily clairvoyant platitudes of the astrologers.

For example, one day two winters ago just east of Toronto's Maple Leaf Gardens, I was accosted by a little old woman who informed me in no uncertain terms that I should be wearing a hat. The woman walked off without another word.

The following winter I was wearing a hat.

Did the little old woman actually foresee that I would be wearing a hat the following winter, or did she intrude in my personal future by planting a suggestion I could not possibly reject? If so, why couldn't I reject it? Had I known the woman's address or telephone number, I might have contacted her this week for an explanation. In her absence, I consulted Sydney Omarr again on Tuesday.

"Be ready for written suggestions," my horoscope told me. "Some will comment 'You look like a different person.' Applaud difference!"

What does "Applaud difference!" mean? Is the horoscope the "written suggestion" I should be ready for? If so, what am I missing?

I was about to get my scissors to clip and save this little brain-teaser from the stars when, just in time, I remembered the warning from the day before about sharp objects.

Sydney and his sinsiter cronies must think I was born yesterday, which would make me a Virgo.

(September 22, 1990)

IS THERE BEER AFTER MARRIAGE?

I can sympathize with the plight of the three-year old American boy who reportedly was scared into constipation by a television commercial that portrayed a toilet as a biting monster. I feel exactly the same way about beer commercials.

I've been so traumatized by beer commercials that just the thought of bringing the neck of a bottle of the stuff to my lips leaves me in a cold sweat.

I'm not sure what the turning point was – whether it was the beer ad with the couple necking ferociously on a fire escape in the rain, the beer ad with the man dancing and preening and mugging to the tune of "Do You Love Me?" in an effort to impress the woman at the bar, or the beer ad that makes fun of the need to be cautious in big cities at night.

One of these and countless other beer commercials in which vigorous attractive young men meet and befriend vigorous, attractive young women has disrupted something in my central nervous system. The result is that I have zero tolerance for beer commercials. I wish the attractive people who live in them but never seem to drink any actual beer would go away forever.

More to the point, I wish the federal government or some other duly-constituted governing body would ban beer commercials. But then, most of the beer commercials are so oblique about the product they're selling that amateurs might have trouble pinpointing the true nature and purpose of the ads.

For instance, is the "Ex says it all" ad campaign a celebration of gruff men who fish and hunt together and smoke too much, or is it a celebration of the brand of beer the people at Molson's would like these men to drink? Where does the ad leave off and the mind-control experiment begin?

* * *

I wonder if all the attractive, single people in beer advertisements continue to drink beer after they marry, settle down and raise a family. No one knows for sure, since married couples are an exceedingly rare phenomenon in beer ads. This could lead us to infer that most people kick the beer habit soon after they get engaged.

Perhaps for this reason, the beer ads tend not to extol the virtues of finding a suitable life companion. The guy who spots the gorgeous blonde sitting at the bar in the exceptionally dumb Labatt's Dry commercial seems to have something slightly less binding than holy matrimony in mind. Ditto that dancing fool in the other brand's ad. Beer-sodden liaisons would seem to be the order of the day.

(A beer ad campaign of the recent past depicted what appeared to be married men gradually going to seed in bucolic places like the Muskokas while their wives humoured them by bringing them the occasional beer. I don't know what became of those poor guys.)

For years, one brand of beer advertised its product by depicting attractive young adults watching a big blue hot-air balloon drift across the sky. That balloon seemed to symbolize ideal happiness, a state of mind altogether lighter than air which might convincingly be simulated by downing a few beers.

The balloon concept has since been dropped, perhaps because many potential customers were inspired to go out and get a life rather than build an imitation of life (a lifestyle, if you will) around the consumption of a specific brand of beer.

The latest commercials for that brand tediously trumpet the beer's new label design, as though we care what the creative staff in marketing have come up with in the way of colours and graphics for their young, affluent target market. Just because they prize form over content doesn't mean we do, no matter how much they'd like us to.

* * *

You never see anyone working or spending quality time with their children in beer commercials. Children do not exist in the universe of beer ads. Neither do parents, by and large. The attractive people in the beer ads seem to have sprung, unencumbered by a genetic rap-sheet of any kind, into a golden world of parties, endless flirtations and desires that are about to be gratified.

I wish I could freeze the TV frame on the average partygoer's refrigerator in the beer ads, then zoom in on it. I bet there's not a single shrivelled baked potato or empty jam jar in that refrigerator.

What's ultimately most horrifying about the world of beer commercials is the utter absence of natural consequences such as coffee-table stains, empties, cigarette burns, garbage, children and having to go to the bathroom.

Speaking of which: The constipated three year old's pediatrician says the boy's family is gently encouraging him to become reacquainted with the toilet and are reassuring him that the toilet is not out to get him.

I wish I felt as sure about that as they do.

(May 12, 1990)

TOURNAMENT OF CELEBRITY DEPOSED RULERS

F. Marcos,
Immediate Past President,
Republic of the Philippines,
Honolulu.

Dindo Gonzales,
Columnist,
Business Day,
Manila.

Dear Mr. Gonzales,

I have been called many things in the weeks since I was illegally stripped of my rightful job as president of the Philippines. My wife, Imelda, has also been called many things by people who don't hold a candle to her when it comes to overall class and good looks.

Misinformed people have called me a tyrant, a despot (which I had to look up in the dictionary) and a thief. Cruel and unfeeling people have made fun of Imelda's 3,000 pairs of shoes, and ridiculed her singing ability. They have accused us of siphoning billions from the Filipino treasury (the actual figure is nowhere near that amount).

People have also questioned my war record. And when I tried to settle all the belly-aching at home by calling a presidential election, they said I rigged that, too. (If it was rigged, how come I'm stuck in Honolulu and Corazon Aquino has my job? Tell me that.)

Imelda and I are used to the wildest libel and slander by now. But never, not even in my wildest dreams, did I think someone would actually stoop so low as you did to accuse me of **cheating at golf.**

Dindo, you little weasel columnist, you've gone too far this time. You think because I'm stuck here in Hawaii I can't get anybody in Manila to lean on you a bit. I've still got a lot of friends back home. You better sit with your back to the wall for the rest of your life, my friend.

I saw in your newspaper column a photocopy of one of my golf scorecards, from December 1978. The card shows that "Pres. F. Marcos" shot a 30 over the first nine holes at the Manila Golf and Country Club. What's so unbelievable about that? I'm an honest golfer. Ask my bodyguards.

In your column, you said when I shot a 30 over nine holes, I "should have turned pro then and there." Let me tell you something, Mister Smart Newspaperman; I applied to the PGA in January, 1979. I even considered handing the presidency over to my son, Ferdinand Jr., to become a golfer full-time and join the pro tour. I figured Imelda could get to sing in some of the best clubs in Vegas while I played celebrity tournaments with Gerry Ford and Bob Hope.

I tried to contact Gary Player, the South African who won the Masters tournament in 1978. He was my inspiration. He shot seven birdies in the last 10 holes of the final round of that tournament. I wanted to say to him "Good shooting, Gary. By the way, do you have any contacts in Sun City for my beautiful wife's singing career?" But I couldn't reach him because he had already left for the Tournament of Champions a week later (which he won) and the Houston Open (which he also won).

I was willing to pay Gary Player an awful lot of money to get Imelda into one of the better clubs in Sun City, and to get me onto the PGA tour – more money than you've ever seen in a lifetime, weasel.

This thing about my bodyguards supposedly kicking my ball out of the rough and into the fairway: I don't know where people like you get your information, but I asked every single one of my bodyguards if they ever did this -- even once -- and they all said "No way, Your Excellency." I asked them did they at any time give any of my balls a more favourable lie. They said, "No way, Your Excellency."

Unlike you, Mister Cynical Newspaperman, I believe what people tell me.

I've been shooting in the mid-30's for years. Just the other day I took out my clubs and played a bit in the compound here in Honolulu. My bodyguards say my stroke is better than ever. I have a lot of time to work on my stroke now – even more time than I had when I was President of the Philippines.

I have been thinking about possibly organizing a big golfing event – a Tournament of Celebrity Deposed Leaders. Someone told me Baby Doc Duvalier knows his way around a golf course. Too bad Somoza got blown up in Paraguay; his nine-iron was the talk of Nicaragua. The Shah was no slouch either. But Idi Amin says he's "go" for the tournament, and that other African, Bokassa, who kept the funny meat in his freezer, is already taking putting lessons in France.

I sent a letter to the government of Costa Rica in April, offering them my tournament and $1 billion in American cash if they'd let me live there. The say Costa Rica is all booked up. The same goes for Spain, Portugal, Italy, Singapore, Indonesia, Panama and most of the West Indies.

So the tournament will have to be in Manila – maybe sometime next year, after I'm back in the palace. I'll be looking for you then, Dindo.

F. Marcos,
Honolulu.

(July 9, 1986)

THE WEATHER IS ALWAYS FOGGY

It's a Sunday night and I'm suffering through a Buffalo TV newscast to catch the day's baseball scores. The weatherwoman has finished explaining the satellite picture of the continent's weather to us, and flashy graphics are now telling us the conditions we can expect during the week. This is what the graphics say:

Mon – Sun and T'shwrs
Tues – Sun and shwrs
Wed – Sun and shwrs

It's the next morning. Rain is falling steadily and the sky is a deep overcast. A man on the FM station solemnly tells us there is a 10-percent possibility of precipitation that day.

Listening to these and other weather reports, it's not hard to notice the similarity between them and the newspaper horoscopes that advise you to "define terms, clarify meaning".

Which terms? What meaning?

In the same way astrologers shelter their professional reputations in sweeping generalizations, today's high-tech weather forecasters cover an awful lot of ground just to cover their behinds.

"Sun and T'shwrs" is not a weather forecast at all. It doesn't help you decide what to wear that day, or whether to get out of bed at all. "Sun and T'shwrs" merely tells you that the people watching the weather haven't the foggiest notion of what to expect, so get off their case and get on with your life.

Which perhaps isn't such bad advice.

There is something rather strange about the daily morning ritual of listening to the weather forecast. After all, thousands of us will spend a mere ten or so minutes outdoors on our way to and from work. The rest of the day will be passed in a climate-controlled building of one sort or another, where nature is shut out.

Here at the *Spectator*, I work in a room of concrete walls painted beige and bright orange. There are no windows. The only time weather intrudes in this room is when a vicious thunderstorm passes overhead, on its way to Burlington. The thunder penetrates the roof of the *Spec* building as a mild thud. When I hear a mild thud, I know I should be seeking shelter if I'm outdoors (which I'm not) and I should be closing windows if I have any (which I don't).

This method of divining the weather is a far cry from the ancient practice of "reading" the clouds and observing the behaviour of fur-bearing animals. Very few people "read" clouds anymore. Perhaps windowless office buildings came into vogue because too many of us were "reading" too many clouds on company time.

As for small fur-bearing animals, they have enough sense to stay away from windowless office buildings, so they're no longer of any use to us.

"Accu-weather" is a relatively recent innovation in media weather forecasting. It seems to involve guessing what the weather might be like over the next several days, so people can plan their flu outbreak in advance.

"Accu-weather" is a misnomer of criminal proportions. When the average weather forecaster can't accurately clue you in on what's going to happen ten minutes from now, guessing the conditions a few days down the road is an impossibility.

To compensate, one of the Toronto TV stations has a weatherman who is able to draw high-pressure systems and write temperatures backwards, with both hands, from behind a glass map. Another Toronto TV station has computer graphics that simulate a sun, some clouds, lightning and even the CN Tower. A third Toronto TV station has a weatherman who feels he must jot down the temperature in every Canadian community with a population in excess of 250.

All of these attention-getting gimmicks are actually attention-diverting gimmicks: "Gee, that guy writes backwards well with both hands. Gee, those computer graphics are neat. Gee, it's cold in Dog's Breath, Labrador." Meanwhile, they hope you're not noticing the local forecast.

In Great Britain, where there's more weather per square kilometre than anywhere else on Earth, the TV forecasters have adapted far better to the situation. They refer to the next day's weather with appropriately foggy adjectives such as "somewhat changeable". Not for them the accu-inaccuracies of "sun and T'shwrs". The Thames could be flowing over the steps of St. Paul's Cathedral and your average U.K. weatherman would admit only that the day has been "damp". He'd rather be mostly cloudy than all wet.

(July 17, 1985)

ALL THE NEWS -- BEFORE IT HAPPENS

The Canadian Broadcasting Corporation, like the other Canadian networks, spent long hours last Saturday filling dead air during the tedious Liberal leadership voting.

Most of us put up with it. We even tried to go along with the networks' pretence that real drama was unfolding from minute to minute.

The CBC's floor reporters were among the greatest pretenders. "Sir, can you tell me where you're throwing your support?" one of them bleated to a candidate while being crushed by a throng of his colleagues shortly after the first-ballot results. The candidate couldn't hear him. "Sir, are you moving towards the Chrétien camp or the Turner camp?"

Had the CBC reporter and all the other reporters simply stood aside to let the candidate go where he was going, he would have arrived there more quickly and the entire nation would have found out what he was doing that much sooner.

But you don't fill dead air that way.

Had I been a candidate, I would have been tempted to get up from my seat, ceremoniously make my way down the aisle to the floor, walk purposefully across the arena and, at the very last minute, tell the reporters I was going to the bathroom.

"Mr. Levesque has decided to throw his support to the men's lavatory," the man from the CBC would be forced to say.

When Mark MacGuigan decided to throw what was left of his support to John Turner, he was almost flattened by people desperate to know in advance what he was doing. Ditto John Munro when he decided to back Jean Chrétien.

Donald Johnston presented a more serious problem for the networks. He refused to throw his support anywhere. Reporters were instructed to watch him closely. "Do I see your left leg beginning to move?" one reporter asked the steadfastly seated Mr. Johnston. "Does this imply that you will soon be standing and eventually putting one leg in front of the other on the way down the stairs to throw your support to another candidate?"

Mr. Johnston couldn't hear him.

Once the second-ballot voting was under way, the situation got positively desperate in terms of the absence of any further support-

throwing speculation. But CBC anchorman Peter Mansbridge had an idea to fill the dead air: Why not shut off all the pundits for a while and let the nation watch the delegates dance on the arena floor?

This they did. The delegates were dancing a modified polka to the strains of "In Heaven There Ain't No Beer."

I imagined a reporter cutting in and breathlessly asking a bouncing delegate, "How much longer do you intend to polka? Does the fact that you are doing the polka mean you decided moments ago to throw your support to–"

Peter Mansbrige cut the reporter off with important news that party president Iona Campagnolo was at the podium. Little did Mr. Mansbridge know that she was there to sing the rousing twenty-third chorus of "In Heaven There Ain't No Beer".

Bleary-eyed, I switched to CTV: Keith Davey's smiling face filled the screen. I quickly switched to Global: Allan Fotheringham's smiling face filled the screen. I switched to CHCH: The Expos were doing battle with the Pirates. I stayed with CHCH for a while.

Once the inevitable Turner victory was confirmed, actual news began to happen at breakneck speed. Mr. Turner promised a press conference in 45 minutes. Finally there was going to be some substance with which to fill the air.

Sure enough, Mr. Turner arrived. After about 10 minutes, CBC broke away from the Prime Minister-designate's inaugural press conference and bade us all a curt goodnight. The CBC threw its support to the ever-gripping *Front Page Challenge*.

I switched to CTV and Global. They weren't covering the press conference either.

I guess the networks got their story, whatever it was.

(June 20, 1984)

JUST ANOTHER PHOTO OPPORTUNITY

You know you're living in Bizarro land when a provincial cabinet minister offers his services as a pin-up boy to a major metropolitan newspaper.

You know this Bizarro land is particularly bizarre when people feel compelled to come to the defence of that cabinet minister.

The idea that Peter Kormos was so publicity-hungry that he had to solicit the *Toronto Sun*, rather than wait patiently for the newspaper to express its interest in him, is a frightening one to consider. After the special glow of being Sunshine Boy wears off, what will Mr. Kormos do next -- swim naked across Lake Ontario?

A maverick politician is one who marches to the beat of his or her own political drum. Aspiring to be a Sunshine Boy does not qualify as the act of a true political maverick.

Pat Nowlan, for better of worse, is a true political maverick. The crusty Tory MP from Nova Scotia, who left his party over its handling of the Meech Lake Accord and the GST, would never dream of asking the Toronto Sun if he could be a Sunshine Boy.

I find this reassuring -- though I have to admit I'm somewhat curious about what Mr. Nowlan would look like in a Tarzan suit.

The question is: Can a provincial consumer minister double as a Sunshine Boy without impairing his performance as a consumer minister?

There are at least two schools of thought on this. One view is that the reason we get so many dullards in politics today is that strict ethical guidelines all but prohibit genuine flakes from applying for the job. Another view is that the reason we got so many flakes in politics today is that the lack of strict ethical guidelines all but prohibits genuine dullards from applying for the job.

I suspect the truth resides somewhere in the middle ground between these two views. Perhaps most of the flakes we see on the political scene nowadays are actually dullards who are mortally afraid of showing their true nature, and vice versa.

It could be that veteran Liberal MP Herb Gray, who is steady as September rain, and almost as exciting, is in fact a wild and crazy guy fighting desperately to keep the outrageous side of his personality under wraps.

Ditto Tory Indian Affairs Minister Tom Siddon. On TV he may look like an acting assistant deputy minister's idea of a matinee idol, but who's to know the kind of wiseacre he is in real life?

America's Gary Hart, on quite the other hand, may have feared he was dull as dishwater, and effectively torpedoed a promising political career by carrying on like a dull-as-dishwater Don Juan.

Remember Mackenzie King, the apparently stolid Prime Minister who saw images of his beloved dog in his shaving lather? If the average Canadian voter had known of King's various supernatural hobbies, how would it have affected their view of him?

For that matter, is the desire to commune with the spirit of one's dog more or less objectionable that the desire to be a Sunshine Boy? This is something we should ponder as Canadian politics enters a new and more volatile phase.

If a political career amounts mainly to a ritualized form of exhibitionism, as some people believe, Peter Kormos may be the most well-adjusted politician in the land, because he knows exactly what the political life offers: an endless series of photo opportunities.

Peter Kormos' greatest error was perhaps that he refused to confine his instinct for being photographed to politically acceptable occasions such as ribbon-cuttings, cheque presentations and natural disasters. Instead he wanted to be appreciated for what he is, which is a guy who wants to be a Sunshine Boy.

There's nothing particularly sexy or sexist about the picture of him the Toronto Sun published. He looks likeable enough, and probably would have made a pleasantly mediocre consumer minister had Premier Bob Rae not felt compelled to dump him.

Then again, having offered himself as a human consumer item for the pleasure of newspaper readers, perhaps Mr. Kormos had some real insights into his cabinet portfolio.

(March 23, 1991)

HOCKEY NIGHT AFTER NIGHT IN CANADA

It's probably an indication of the sorry current state of national unity that not all Canadians are convinced 40 nights of Stanley Cup hockey on our public television airwaves is the ideal way to bind the country through the uncertain spring of 1991.

I can't think of a more useful outlet for asserting our nationhood at this point than to watch hearty Canadian boys (plus some Americans, plus some Russians, plus some Czechs, plus some Swedes, plus some Finns) chase a small black rubber disc along an artificial ice surface. Next to back bacon and Paul Anka, hockey is our most successful export.

Instead of bemoaning the seemingly endless series of hockey games on the CBC, we should celebrate the endurance of this rough-hewn sport as it carries us relentlessly toward the summer solstice. Unlike the fate of nations, the seasons are as permanent and unchanging in the cosmic scheme of things as the chip on Don Cherry's shoulder.

Besides, hockey best reflects the basic realities of Canadian life: plenty of ice, relatively small goals and two minutes for holding.

* * *

I must confess I'm one of those fair-weather fans who ignore the NHL's pointless 80-game regular season and start tuning into the annual hockey wars in April, when games actually count for something.

Because of this, I can at least partly identify with those Canadians who believe hockey as a whole is pointless, and who resent having their favourite prime-time programs pre-empted night after night by *Hockey Night After Night In Canada*.

Thanks to recent advances in television technology, however, the deprivation is not as harsh as it once was. With a handy cordless cable converter in hand, it's possible to switch effortlessly to one's best-loved evening soap during the alarmingly frequent commercial interruptions of the hockey game, or vice versa.

Some of the newer TVs can even display two separate channels onscreen simultaneously. Thus as J.R. Ewing put the gun to his head in the allegedly concluding episode of *Dallas*, one could have watched the Bruins and Penguins go at it on a mini-screen in the corner of the big screen.

The beauty of technology is that it's almost as good at solving problems as it is at creating them.

* * *

Given the sheer length of time over which they unfold, some the Stanley Cup playoffs, like life itself, meander inconclusively from one period to the next. When this happens, even the most passionate hockey fan is grateful for the power of the little converter to scan the whole cable-TV spectrum for worthwhile stimulus.

For example, last Sunday evening, while the Penguins were subduing the Bruins, I found myself switching regularly to other stations during the commercials. By the start of the third period, I was flicking the converter whenever the referee's whistle sounded, regardless of whether an ad was imminent.

Before long, I was paying equal attention to the hockey game and a PBS special marking the 100th anniversary of Carnegie Hall. Beverly Sills and Peter Jennings provided colour commentary for the gala event in the celebrated New York concert hall.

As the third period of the Bruins-Penguins match dragged on, I began to spend more time at Carnegie Hall than in the Pittsburgh arena. It occurred to me that I was possibly the only person on earth experiencing these two events at the same time. I wondered if this was something I ought to be proud of.

When conductor Zubin Mehta mounted the podium to dedicate the glorious finale of Mahler's third symphony to the late Leonard Bernstein, I abandoned the hockey game altogether and watched in awe as the members of the New York Philharmonic executed the fundamentals, gave 110 per cent and finished all their checks.

If only Danny Gallivan had been on hand to give the play-by-play.

(May 11, 1991)

4.

HORROR STORIES FROM HOME

WHOSE HOSE IS IT, ANYWAY?

As the vernal equinox looms and various species of spring flowers poke their tender head through the soil in sunny residential beds, a single question burns in my mind: Should I finally take the garden hose in for the winter?

There was an undetermined moment, probably some time in the month of February, when the notion of physically going out and carrying the garden hose down to the basement became at least as nonsensical as the notion of not getting around to taking the hose in at all.

I didn't consciously delay dealing with the hose. In the dead of winter, whenever it occurred to me that I should bring that blasted hose in from the cold before it cracks and bursts, other chores, like listening to music or wrestling with the cat, invariably took precedence.

I remember one sunny, mild day in early January when I seriously resolved to go out and get the hose. But then I noticed that my wife had just washed the floors. I couldn't in all conscience drag a dirty muddy hose over those pristine floors.

Then in the middle of the month, the Gulf War broke out and nothing got done around the house. Instead, we spent endless hours in front of the TV, looking at colour maps of the Persian Gulf with fuzzy photos of news correspondents telling us, through the staticky line of a satellite telephone hook-up, what they were looking at outside their window.

Meanwhile, outside my own window, the garden hose lay forgotten and unattended.

* * *

Over the course of the days, weeks and months in which my garden hose has languished at the side of the house, my wife had at least as many opportunities as I did to put it away for the winter.

I didn't see her out there in the cold, detaching the hose from the faucet with a wrench. I didn't hear her once say she would bring the hose in. For some reason, it's assumed I'm the one who brings in the hose when the snow flies.

Forgive me if I sound defensive, but where is it written that the man always has custody of the hose?

Sometimes I wish there was a number in the Yellow Pages I could call to pay someone to come over and put the hose away for me. I feel especially ashamed because, prior to this year, the latest I ever got around to putting the hose away was early February, when there was still a sizeable chunk of winter left to live through.

This year, though, the hose sits out there as mute testament to my entire failure as a man and a homeowner. I don't even have the heart to go out and check on its physical condition. I am criminally negligent.

* * *

As March marches onward into April, my abandoned hose has become an albatross around my neck. If I were a character in ancient mythology, I would have flung myself off the nearest cliff by now to put an end to my anguish.

Before throwing myself from the cliff, I would have been tormented by visions of dragging the hose down to the basement, like Sisyphus, only to have to drag it back out of the house to water the parched lawn in July, only to have to drag it back into the house to shelter it from the icy winds of early January, and so on and on.

In my vision, the months would pass with the speed of pages being torn from a wall calendar, night would follow day in the wink of an eye, seasons would blur into one another, and the only unchanging force in the entire universe would be that wretched garden hose of mine, waiting by the side of the house for its owner to deal with it.

But these are the 1990s, not ancient mythology. I hereby declare my independence from my garden hose. As of this moment, that hose is responsible for its own welfare. If, in the years to come, I occasionally get around to using or maintaining it, so be it. If not, so be it. The hose is on its own from this day forward.

Having gotten that off my chest, I think I may yet work up the courage to go out and take a quick look at the hose, preferably under the cover of darkness, to prove I'm not a complete monster.

(March 9, 1991)

GROSS DOMESTIC PRODUCT

In this superficially antiseptic post-industrial world of ours, it's always instructive to be reminded of the mess we leave behind on a daily basis as we move through life.

At least, this is what I'm telling myself in a futile attempt to lighten the psychological blow of a bill for recent repairs to the sewage drainage system in the basement of my home.

Up until last weekend, I had no idea where the water from the toilet, shower and sundry sinks in the house flowed before interfacing with the great network of underground pipe that carries the city's waste to the central holding tank, also known as Lake Ontario.

Not only did I not know where our household waste water went, I didn't feel the least bit curious about it. My philosophy, up until last weekend, was to leave the intricacies of domestic sewage to plumbers and other professional practitioners who, after all, are handsomely rewarded for their devotion to the topic.

The price of my disinterest was driven home to me a week ago today when, on one of my rare visits to the basement, I happened to notice that everyting our household plumbing was designed to carry unseen and unsmelled to some faraway place was streaming across the basement floor in a perverse detour from its appointed route.

This sewage crisis occasioned a house call by a company that specializes in the less than glamorous nuts and bolts of this science. The man from the company brought with him a nifty little electrical machine that pumps a length of coiled metal with blades on the end deep into the otherwise inaccessible reaches of the house's intestinal system. This decepively simple machine effectively reams the sewer pipes, dislodging any foreign substances.

After several extensions of coiled metal are attached to it, the little sewer-reamer can actually blaze a subterranean trail right out to the street, where the household pipes spill into the much larger, theoretically unpluggable municipal sewer pipes.

What happened this day, to the mild consternation of the otherwise sublimely unflappable man from the sewage company, is that the first length of coiled metal became stuck in my pipe.

"Does that pipe run out to your weeping tiles?" the man asked me. I stalled for time by kneading my forehead. The simple fact was that I had absolutely no idea what weeping tiles were, let alone where they might be located.

"Could be," I said finally, thinking to myself how odd it is that you're given complex operation manuals for inconsequential things like toaster-ovens and blenders, whereas you're expected to wade into home ownership entirely on your own, without even a single instruction sheet.

In all the years I spent in a futile wrestling match with algebra in high school, I don't recall a teacher once mentioning weeping tiles. Why do you suppose that is?

Maybe if we understood in precise detail the intricate infrastructure of a house and the seemingly countless ways it can break down, we'd all be renting furnished apartments from the cradle to the grave to avoid all that needless aggravation.

On the other hand, a core meltdown in one's household sewage-disposal system is an object lesson in environmental chaos. You come away from such a crisis with a drastically raised ecological consciousness, not to mention an irresistible urge to hose yourself down.

Ironically, one of the reasons the world's environmental problems have become so acute is that we've so efficiently insulated ourselves from them. We don't know what the toxic grunge on the floor of Burlington Bay looks like. We don't often go on picnics at landfill sites. We insist that dog-owners clean up after their pets in public parks even as we remain ignorant of who or what is cleaning up after us.

As you can plainly see, the wisdom I've gained over the past week far outweighs the few hundred dollars it cost me.

(August 17, 1991)

DROWNING IN A SEA OF HULA HOOPS

How can there be room in the world for everything?

This question arose in my mind as a result of a remark my wife made. Her remark arose as a result of watching me spend the better part of five hours raking leaves from our yard and throwing them into the surrounding woods.

She said: "Just think of all the layers of leaves that have accumulated through the ages."

I was not overly disposed at the time to "just think" of anything to do with leaves. I was too busy trying to figure out how foliage from several surrounding acres routinely finds its way into my yard in the fall.

Every winter, I sit by the window and trust the snow and cold will mulch all those leaves into microscopic bits of food for the grass. But this never happens. Instead, the snow acts like formaldehyde. Come April, the leaves are as good as new, lying all over the place, choking the young grass to death.

My lawn mower is not programmed to mulch. It's barely programmed to mow. I believe I mistakenly purchased a lawn *flattener* rather than a mower, per se. So in spring I rake and rake and rake, and throw and throw and throw the leaves into the surrounding bush.

The first law of thermodynamics tells us that the weight of the materials entering into any reaction must be exactly equal to the weight of materials to be accounted for when the reaction has been completed.

So where do the leaves go?

"The leaves break down," my daughter informed us. "They return to the soil in the form of nutrients and continue the natural life cycle of the wilderness."

I wondered if it was because of this awareness of the natural life cycle of the wilderness that my daughter never volunteers to disrupt it by helping rake the bloody leaves out of the yard.

I further wondered why the leaves don't consent to do their breaking down right in the yard over the winter, thereby sparing me the labour of moving them to another final resting place.

"It takes longer than that for the leaves to break down," my daughter scoffed.

"From now on," I muttered to my wife, "they'll be given all the time they need."

In the meantime, having begun the job of clearing the yard of leaves, I was compelled to finish, if only for the sake of appearances. The task made me morose.

I pondered the concept of garbage incinerators that merely turn solid trash into gaseous trash. I pondered the frightening concept that *nothing ever really goes away*. As soon as we produce anything in this civilization, we're stuck with it, for keeps.

As with any repetitive form of exertion, raking soon induces a trance-like state in which cockamamey notions pass themselves off as epiphanies. I began to wonder where all the discarded hula hoops in the world are stored, and what good there was in trying to discard anything in an orderly, businesslike fashion, when things quite simply don't allow themselves to be discarded.

As I raked my way to a bed of water-logged leaves piled up against the back of the house, I had a vision of Earth a few hundred years from now: Archaeologists in jumpsuits made of aluminum foil are excavating the precise site where I have been raking all these years. After considerable digging they reach a level of leaves. They dig further. More leaves. They dig and dig, and leaves are all they encounter.

They conclude, from the absence of anything but leaves, that there was no human presence on this site between the 18th and 21st centuries. Digging further, the archaeologists discover there was once a village of Indians, who obviously had the good sense not to bother trying to clean up after nature.

(April 25, 1984)

THE BLUE BOX BLUES

Our household has developed a symbiotic relationship with the people who design, print and deliver the various advertising flyers that find their way into our mailbox. I believe this relationship is a particularly good example of how people can work together to make the world a better place. It goes like this:

The carriers drop the flyers into our mailbox, usually on Sunday. I open my front door, lean over to scoop the flyers out of the mailbox, and immediately drop them into the blue recycling box sitting just next to the door on my front porch. I then carry the box out to the front of the yard, where it gets picked up the following morning. The paper is then recycled and perhaps even sold to the people who designed, printed and delivered the flyers and the cycle starts all over again.

Isn't that beautiful?

I'm at a loss to name the companies who advertise in the flyers that are delivered to our home. I'm far too interested in recycling to bother reading them. But somebody must be reading them, otherwise the companies would have long ago ceased to advertise this way. Or, like the real-estate people who would like to appraise the market value of our home free of charge and at our convenience, they would have adopted an advertising medium that more closely resembles a letter or something you might even be remotely interested in fishing out of your mailbox.

I think some of the people who deliver the flyers are wise to my instant recycling methods. At least one carrier has taken to stuffing his flyer under the pot of mums that used to sit at the edge of the verandah (somebody ripped them off last weekend). That way I don't hear his footsteps on the verandah stairs and I don't see the flyer when I peer out the door.

Occasionally, another carrier wedges his flyer between the slats at the front of the verandah. This of course exposes the flyer to any rain that might happen to be falling, and a moderate gust of wind is usually sufficient to dislodge the flyer and blow it the short distance eastward to our little hedge, against which (with any luck) it unfurls and impales itself, as though it had been thumbtacked there by an especially neat and industrious vandal.

Every couple of weeks, my eyes dart over a brand name or company logo as I remove the soggy advertising flyers, chocolate bar wrappers, potato chip bags, fast food hamburger containers, bubble-gum papers, tufts of Kleenex, cigarette-package cellophane, small white plastic bags, popsicle sticks, aluminum cans and other disposable items from my tiny front yard.

It's not with any particular rancour that I retrieve the errant advertising flyers from my yard. I figure they were placed there with a certain responsible pre-meditation – even if it was on the misguided assumption that I wanted to read the damned things – while the rest of the detritus has been deposited in my yard without an iota of consideration for my feelings.

The difference between a soggy advertising flyer lying in the mud under my hedge and a potato-chip bag pasted to the trunk of my little Japanese maple is the difference between night and an exceptionally dark day: One is deliberate garbage, the other is indifferent garbage. Guess which is which.

* * *

I suppose if I didn't want all those advertising flyers in my mailbox and elsewhere on my property, I could contact the relevant authorities and ask that my home be omitted from that carrier's route.

Or I could affix a little sign to my mailbox that says:

DON'T PUT ANYTHING IN HERE THAT DOESN'T HAVE A STAMP ON IT (UNLESS IT'S ANYTHING FROM THE SWEEPSTAKES DEPARTMENT OF READER'S DIGEST, WHICH SHOULD NEVER BE PUT IN HERE EVEN IF IT DOES HAVE A STAMP ON IT (UNLESS THE OUTSIDE OF THE ENVELOPE CLEARLY INDICATES THAT THE OCCUPANT HAS WON A MAJOR SWEEPSTAKE PRIZE (IN WHICH CASE I'D LIKE TO KNOW WHAT RIGHT YOU HAVE TO READ MY PRIVATE MAIL?)))

Or I could use my blue recycling box as my mailbox, and sort the phone bills and credit-card invoices from the A&P flyers whenever the spirit moved me – assuming the spirit ever moved me.

(October, 15, 1988)

YOUR SOCKS ARE IN ATLANTIS

The age-old mystery of what happens to some socks after they're put in the dryer appears to have been solved.

My wife discovered the other day that the static electricity generated by the dryer had caused a stray sock to vanish up the legs of an old pair of track pants. This discovery quickly led to the formulation of a general theory which may finally explain a phenomenon that has puzzled the world for generations.

My wife hypothisized that some pairs of track pants – especially old and unattractive pairs bought in the heyday of track apparel, when people actually thought they looked good in them – often languish at the bottom of a dresser drawer for months at a time with the stray socks trapped in them.

These seldom-worn track pants finally come out of the drawer long after the missing sock's useless matching sock has been chucked into the garbage or converted to shoe or furniture-polishing duty, which means the newly found sock now serves no purpose, either.

The sad fact is that when a sock enters into this kind of self-destructive symbiotic relationship with a pair of track pants, there is little hope of rehabilitating it.

* * *

Would it be possible for the occasional sock to vanish into other items of clothing or a fabric of some kind?

Yes, says my wife. A sock could affix itself to a tablecloth, which the owner then unwittingly folds and stores away. Or it could adhere to a flannel sheet that is being put away for the summer.

Short of increasing the amount of fabric softener in the drying cycle, is there any other way of preventing the random loss of single socks?

One solution might be to wash the socks in their paired state by creating those cute little bulb-shaped sock couplets that are made by placing one sock against the other and turning them inside out together.

The problem with coupled socks, of course, is that they won't dry as well. Also, there's still a risk, albeit a significantly reduced one, that the pair of socks will attach itself to the inner leg of track pants. What further compounds the problem in these cases is that a missing pair of socks is a lot less conspicuous than a missing single sock when you're tallying up your laundry.

* * *

For years, the most common explanation of the disappearing sock phenomenon was that they had an arrangement with coat-hangers whereby they changed places with individual coat-hangers in a parallel universe, which would explain the often alarming proliferation of coat-hangers in our own universe.

I never seriously subscribed to this sock/coat-hanger scenario, mainly because I doubted either socks or coat-hangers were sufficiently sentient objects to cook up any kind of conscious conspiracy, or that they would possess the sophisticated knowledge necessary to move at will from one universe to another.

That leaves us with the problem of where all those extra coat-hangers come from. Do dry-cleaning companies secretly stuff a few extra hangers into each batch of cleaned clothes to alleviate the serious over-supply of hangers on their own premises? If so, where did all the extra hangers come from in the first place?

Could those hangers be artifacts from the ancient sunken civilization of Atlantis – complex implements whose origin and purpose have been lost in the mists of time? Would Atlanteans laugh out loud if they saw the lowly use to which we put their once-exalted hangers? It's a question that could use answering.

Let us go even further and suppose that the Atlantean coat-hangers are in fact a sophisticated anti-static device that prevented Atlantean socks from travelling up the legs of Atlantean track pants? Has anyone ever tried throwing a coat hanger into the dryer with a load of wash? I'm going downstairs right now to give it a try.

(December 8, 1990)

5.

A SERIES OF MORAL DILEMMAS

ON HEARING OF BEN JOHNSON AT SEOUL

On a brief visit to my ancestral home in Northern Ontario last weekend, I was suprised to discover that one of the Elysian fields on which I played as a youngster has become the new headquarters of Ontario's Ministry of Correctional Services. The symbolic implications were unsettling, to say the least.

I had several playing fields to choose from within the city limits of North Bay in my childhood days. But this one, on the grounds of the imposingly silver-domed Normal School – later renamed Teacher's College – was my favourite. No one seemed to use it except my friend Marcel and I.

As dictated by the intangible seasons of sport, we variously hit flies and grounders, flew balsa-wood glider planes propelled by elastic bands or played our own unusual game of kick-football on that oddly shaped patch of green in the heart of town. It was our private playground.

At that age, I dreamed of a professional career as a punter/place-kicker. There was something wonderfully cathartic about kicking the daylights out of a football – perhaps angling it to land among the dry brittle leaves the maintenance people thoughtfully heaped in a far corner of the field.

Marcel and I kicked the football back and forth for hours on end. We seldom condescended to throw it, perhaps because neither of us could throw as far as we could kick. Self-esteem counts for an awful lot when you're a kid.

Back then, I took particular pride in my ability to punt the football high in the air. The ball hung up in the sky for what seemed like an eternity, spiralling in a dramatic parabola just like the professionals' kicks. Marcel usually was able to kick the ball farther than I did, but I preferred to calculate distance by altitude. I sometimes imagined I could kick the ball into orbit if I practised hard and dedicated myself to the art.

Place-kicking was a lot more difficult to master. When the people from the ministry of correctional services first inspected their new construction site, they probably wondered why the field was indented with so many tiny craters. I could have explained to them that the craters were made by the heel of my left foot, digging places to stand the football on end for the purpose of place-kicking it, with any luck, into Marcel's end-zone. The better the crater, the more height and distance I got out of the ball.

Over time, I became reasonably adept at place-kicking. By age 12, I figured I was destined for a career with the CFL. The kicker's life seemed perfect: plenty of rest between work stints, minimal contact with 300-pound linemen and the prospect of glory in the dying seconds of a close game.

My fantasies about a CFL career were of course far-flung. Marcel was as good at place-kicking as I was, and it was hard even for a 12-year-old to imagine both he and his best friend were future Hall of Famers.

To sustain my fantasy, I decided I had to become better than Marcel at place-kicking. One Saturday morning, on one of my regular visits to the sporting-goods section of the local Canadian Tire, I found the solution: a small plastic kicking tee.

For the rest of that summer, I dominated our place-kicking contests with my little tee. The ball soared time after time through the imaginary uprights. Marcel often complained that my best kicks were wind-assisted, or that the tee made the competition unfair. What most bothered him was that my kicks routinely sailed out of the field altogether, into the parking lot beyond his end-zone.

"Go get your own tee if you're so jealous," I would say to him. But he never did, and our games gradually became less frequent. Soon, I found myself more often than not alone on the field of Teacher's College, kicking the ball farther and farther with the help of my tee, moving relentlessly and by myself toward some imagined pinnacle of glory.

Sic transit gloria mundi, a clever Roman said a couple of millenia ago. I don't know what ever became of that little plastic tee, I don't even own a football anymore, and now the government is putting up an office building on that Elysian field of glory.

This nags at me: What I remember most vividly about those times is not the unofficial 40-yard field goals I kicked by myself with the help of the tee. I remember the earlier days instead, those excellent hours Marcel and I spent staving off puberty and the awesome throes of adulthood by playing together with no particular purpose under the big northern sky.

Even a solo competitor is a member of a team – the group with which he or she plays the game. A basic code of fairness, written and unwritten, applies to every player. I broke the code of our game that summer, so many years ago, by blindly pursuing personal excellence with a little plastic tee. I forgot what the game was about. Sometimes I think we've all forgotten.

(October 1, 1988)

THE BEGGAR OF BLOOR STREET

The strip of Toronto's Bloor Street between Yonge and Bathurst contains some of the most expensive real estate in Canada. As if to reflect this, the man who begged for money at the corner of Bay and Bloor looked somewhat more affluent than his colleagues on other street corners.

He didn't seem to be having much luck with the lunch-hour crowd streaming in and out of their office towers. Standing in a blinding wedge of sunlight at the foot of the imposing ManuLife Centre as a mild September wind mussed his longish hair, the beggar asked for spare change. His appeals were mostly ignored or rebuffed.

Seeing a beggar on this strip of Bloor Street is unsettling for a variety of reasons: We don't like to have our privacy invaded while we walk purposefully to a lunch date or meeting. We don't like to be forced into the moral discomfort of turning down someone who demonstrably needs something. And, most important of all, we hate to be reminded that, amid the often grotesque displays of plenty in the city, some of the people who live here don't have enough.

I sat on a low concrete wedge and, contentedly eating a hot dog I had purchased at one of those outdoor trolleys that dot the main intersections of the city, watched the beggar ply his trade.

He didn't look like someone who was abusing drugs or alcohol. He was in his mid to late-20s, and didn't appear to be in bad physical shape. So what was he doing at the corner of Bay and Bloor on this bright afternoon: supplementing his welfare cheque? making ends meet between cheques? researching a sociology term paper?

As I wiped mustard from the corner of my mouth, a young businessman produced some change from his pocket and, without breaking his stride, dropped the money into the beggar's out-stretched palm. I don't think I've ever witnessed a more perfunctory or impersonal act of charity.

The majority of the passers-by ignored the beggar altogether, but he knew better than to harass anyone about it. He'd get pulled off the street in a flash if he ever harassed anybody. But you could see the resentment on the face of some of the people who hurried by this inconvenient man with his inconvenient out-stretched palm.

In this affluent and relentlessly materialistic society, there is sometimes an unconscious tendency to disbelieve poverty – to conclude that people who do without necessities such as a square meal or a roof over their head are guilty of self-deprivation, that they have brought their poverty upon themselves.

So there is sometimes an unconscious resentment of the poor for having crashed our party and forced us, if only for a moment, to consider the even more dramatic economic injustices that are a fact of global life.

In short, poor people are a downer.

I had finished my hot dog. Now came the task of deciding whether I was going to cross the beggar's path, and whether I was going to give him any money.

* * *

The previous evening on Yonge Street just north of Bloor, I had been stopped by a beggar who said he wanted money for a meal. I was walking to a nearby theatre. "Sorry," I said to him.

"So you're not going to help me out?" he said, without bitterness.

I kept walking.

A couple of minutes later, overcome by shame, I retraced my path in search of the beggar who had stopped me. I wanted to give him a couple of dollars so he could go for a hamburger or something. I knew full well I was doing it only to salve my own conscience, but I wanted to do it anyway.

I never did find him.

And now, as I walked toward the beggar of Bay-Bloor, I saw that he had retreated from his wedge of sunlight into the shade. He was seated, carefully counting his coins.

I began walking more quickly. As I swept by him, I handed him a dollar. "Do something right with it," I said.

I don't know what I meant by that arrogant remark, or why I imagined I was entitled to say it to him. A steady income keeps hunger at bay, but all the money in the world doesn't buy an ounce of righteousness.

(September 24, 1988)

ARE WE LOVING WHALES TO DEATH?

People who are especially fond of looking at whales are not especially fond of people who hunt and harpoon whales.

Even I, who never had the good fortune to lay eyes on a whale in the wild, must confess that whale-killers are not often on my party guest list.

Leave the whales alone, I say. Let them peacefully ply the waters and sing their interminable sea chanteys that are comprehensible only to their felllow whales and the odd gifted dolphin.

My sympathy for the plight of the whale community derives from the fact that, given their ample size, they are easily the biggest visible minority on the planet. I don't deplore their slaughter because they're cute. An animal that's larger than a Mack truck hardly qualifies for cuteness. I deplore it because I believe we are capable of enjoying life just as much without having to prey on these blubbery beasts.

Smugly I have preached that it's far better for both us and the whales to shoot them with a loaded Pentax. A lot of people share that view. The whale-watching industry is booming – so much so that naturalists now say we're driving the whales crazy with our boats and cameras.

Last year, more than 75,000 people paid for day excursions from Providence, Rhode Island alone -- for the sole purpose of watching whales. "We have no idea what we're doing to the mental state of these animals," says marine naturalist Steven Morello. "We maybe should start using our heads a little."

Let's use our heads, then: Let's put ourselves in the shoes of the whale, who's attempting to go about his daily routine in his aquamarine environment, but must constantly dodge excursion boats full of human gawkers. " What is it with these humans," the whale might ask himself. "Half of them are out to kill me, the other half want to love me to death".

Mr. Morello says whale-watchers have disrupted the whales' feeding and mating habits. There's a tremendous irony here, if his assessment is correct. And there's a lesson, too. I think what he is trying to say on behalf of the whales is that the open sea is not a zoo. Or, better yet: How would you like alien animals to come into your home every day and disrupt your feeding and mating habits?

The problem boils down to this: Now that so many people have developed a healthy, benevolent attitude toward whales, how does one go about quenching this admirable human interest without disrupting the whales' lives?

For starters, we might consider camouflaging whale-watching excursion boats as freight vessels. Should a whale be spotted, passengers diguised as wooden crates would be instructed to observe the whales only out of the corner of their eyes.

Or, to reassure the whales, decoy excursion boats could be sent out for the specific purpose of NOT encountering and NOT observing whales. Should such a boat come within 500 metres of a whale, it would immediately speed off in the opposite direction.

Failing that, the minds behind the mechanical shark in the movie *Jaws* could be hired by the govenrnment to secretly design and build a convoy of mechanical whales which could be installed off the Eastern seaboard for the amusement and edification of tourists. Maintenance costs easily could be covered by a fraction of the proceeds from the excursion fee.

And if none of these ideas works, qualified marine specialists could be enlisted to disguise the whales as oil slicks, which interest no one.

Of course, there is a chance the naturalists' concern is misplaced: Perhaps the whales are watching us.

(June 27, 1984)

ZEN AND THE ART OF DYING

If your annual personal tax bill were $22.4 million, you'd probably consider having your $83-million Van Gogh painting cremated alongside you, if only to spite the tax department and all the other people who forever reminded you that you can't take it with you.

The fact is you *can* take it with you. It just isn't worth anything where you're going.

Japanese pulp and paper magnate Ryoei Saito, the man with the world's largest personal tax bill, created an international stir a few days ago when he made an offhand remark to reporters that he might want to have his Van Gogh and Renoir paintings sealed into his coffin and cremated with him after he dies. He acquired the two paintings at auctions last spring for a total of $161 million.

Mr. Saito later explained to the world that he intended the remark as a kind of Buddhist joke, inspired by the ages-old belief that it's a good idea to bring your favourite things with you to the grave. As an example, he referred to the recently-unearthed army of terra cotta soldiers and horses buried with China's Emperor Qin Shi Huangdi.

The purely legal fact of the matter is that if Mr. Saito wants to use his Van Gogh and his Renoir as dartboards, he's fully entitled to do so. But I don't think the world likes to be reminded of that.

* * *

We all possess favourite things – art objects, trinkets, hockey cards, etc. – we would be hard pressed to part with. The only consolation the poor have when thinking about the rich is that the latter have a whole lot more they eventually have to give up.

For someone as fabulously wealthy as Mr. Saito, who buys virtually priceless works of art the way you and I might purchase a new refrigerator, the problem of separating himself from his personal possessions will be enormous.

My mother, who grew up during the Depression, never tires of explaining how her generation had almost nothing when they were kids. They barely had enough food to go around, let alone toys or spending money.

My mother and her socio-economic peers "did without" as she puts it. The implication is that by "doing without" they developed a solid disposition, learned not to fear "a little hard work" and cultivated a healthy skepticism about the actual value of material things.

The subtext of my mother's memory of her own childhood is that kids today have so much, they can no longer distinguish between what they want and what they need.

If that's the case, consider the predicament of Mr. Saito, pulp-and-paper baron, who pays more personal tax in one year than you and I can hope to earn in a lifetime. How do you think he feels about dying?

* * *

A recent Elvis Costello song astutely observed that it was a millionaire, John Lennon, who urged us to imagine no possessions.

Most rich people probably enjoy being rich, though I'm not aware of any recent opinion surveys on the topic. But for some, the accumulation of material wealth eventually becomes a kind of albatross around their nicely-tanned neck, a tether that binds them to the material world.

You and I can look at Van Gogh's paintings in a book, or even admire them in museums here and there in the world. But only people in Mr. Saito's socio-economic sphere have to worry about what to do with the damn things after they die.

What Mr. Saito did last week was to muse out loud about how he would dispose of his Van Gogh and Renoir after he's gone. A lot of people were not amused. The seemed to think – and even Mr. Saito eventually expressed roughly the same view – that such works of art belong to the whole world.

Symbolically, these paintings belong to us all. But in material terms, they are just another commodity to be acquired and disposed of at the whim of the highest bidders.

Vincent Van Gogh, who died penniless and wasn't able to sell a single painting in his lifetime, would have been in the best position to savour the irony of Mr. Saito's little dilemma.

(May 18, 1991)

GREATEST HITS OF THE WAR

In my adolescence, K-Tel was known primarily as the purveyor of TV-advertised collections of recent pop-music hits. These K-Tel albums, breathlessly pitched in TV ads by an overexcited male voice, had predictable titles like *Hot Hits* and *Groovy Greats* and inevitably offered several samples of chaff along with the wheat.

Not having watched a whole lot of television in the 1980s, I'm not sure what became of those periodic K-Tel albums. For all I know they just kept coming, with more up-to-date titles like *Punk Power* and *Rap Rave-Up*.

One way or the other, I was surprised the other day to find myself staring at a K-Tel ad on television. The ad featured an overexcited male voice running through the unbelievable attractions available at a special introductory price, or some such spiel.

The product K-Tel was pitching this time was not a vinyl record, which everyone in the music industry has dropped like a hot potato, but a video cassette. The title of the video cassette was *Operation Desert Storm*.

It became obvious very early on in the commercial that we were to think of K-Tel's new product as a kind of greatest hits of the Gulf war – an invaluable memento to relive again and again those special moments in the Persian Gulf when coalition forces smote the lowly Iraqi.

Call it the mother of all marketing strategies: a pre-emptive spiel in which we are urged to buy a video about the war before we've quite made up our mind about what exactly transpired in the Persian Gulf in January and February of this year.

Instead of listing smash hits by the likes of Gary Puckett And The Union Gap, K-Tel's ad for its Operation Desert Storm video runs through some of the highlights we can look forward to cherishing for years to come:

- See Patriot missiles intercept and destroy incoming Scud missiles, sometimes without causing any casualties at all.
- See the latest generation of smart bombs thread the needle of enemy fortifications as they relentlessly home in on their strategic target.
- See the mighty Tomahawk cruise missile on its unerring course from its ship-based launching pad to suburban Baghdad.

- See the mysterious Stealth bomber, secret weapon of the coalition, as it leaves on yet another classified mission over enemy territory.
- See the night skyline of Baghdad light up like a pinball machine under coalition bombardment.
- See enemy casualties by the tens of thousands. (On second thought, skip that one.)

What's perhaps most stunning about the K-Tel war video is that anyone who spent those terrible hours glued to their television sets a few weeks ago would even dream of owning a commemorative video that gives them yet another peek into the jaws of Hell.

Since there is no law against living off the avails of war, companies like K-Tel are entirely within their rights to compile a quickie video of the conflict and flog it to the public.

Before the war was over, a line of Desert Storm cards was already on the market for collectors not sufficiently amused by the increasingly valuable cards from the world of sport. ("I'll trade you my dead Iraqi civilian for your dead Kuwaiti civilian.")

Even as Kuwait slowly moves back to its pre-invasion semblance of "liberation" and begins cleaning up the obscene mess left by the forces of Saddam Hussein, and even as Iraq descends into post-war bloodletting and political mayhem, we in the West are having the Gulf war neatly packaged and marketed as a kind of entertainment worthy of an evening's diversion from the everyday trials of life.

Despite this era of instant electronic information, we have no stomach for what war is actually about. K-Tel's greatest hits of the Gulf war, like much of the news about the war itself, will show us the shiny, reassuring tip of an enormous and very ugly iceberg – the only part of it that's at all marketable.

(March 30, 1991)

AN INCIDENT IN TERMINAL 2

One evening last week, a man attacked a woman with a knife. The event itself is fairly common in the complex fabric of a big city. What made this incident uncommon was the fact that it occurred in Terminal 2 of Toronto's Pearson International Airport, just a few feet away from where I was standing.

I don't know, and probably never will know, the particulars of the incident. I have no idea what the attacker's motive was, and whether his victim, a woman in her mid-twenties, was known to him.

Was he trying to rob the woman, settle a personal account, or merely projecting his personal rage and desperation onto an unknown passerby who had the misfortune to encounter him at the precise moment when his impotence crystallized into violence?

Shortly after the incident, I watched a woman, clutching what appeared to be a couple of boarding passes, lead the victim down the main terminal corridor away from the scene of the crime. She had been slashed in the hand. The blood from it was surprisingly bright-red, almost artificial. She was in a state of shock.

Meanwhile, her assailant sat on the floor against the wall around the corner from the main corridor, near an elevator. A man, another passerby just like me, had pinned him there.

For a couple of minutes that evening, in a place customarily filled with coming and going, it was as though several of us had been nailed to the floor.

* * *

A genuine scream of horror has a different effect than the screams you hear in the movies and on TV. The fact that it comes out of the blue, without preparatory hints such as tense music and odd camera angles, further deepens the shock of someone's unexpected anguish.

The scream I heard that evening at the airport was vivid and very close. I was killing time in a bookstore when it pierced the hubbub of passengers and their friends and relatives. It was sudden distress made vocal, and it chilled the blood. What struck me afterward was the reflexive way so many people immediately responded to it.

I was maybe the third or fourth person on the scene. The woman was still struggling with her assailant. "He's got a knife," someone had the presence of mind to cry out. I have no idea how many seconds or fractions of seconds had passed when I saw the knife slide toward me on the floor. It came to rest at the feet of the man in front of me.

"Get the knife," I said to no one in particular. That's when the man in front of me decided to wedge it under his shoe. It was a black handled kitchen knife – the kind you might use to chop celery. The victim fled around the corner and someone knocked the attacker down. The struggle had been strangely silent, then it stopped altogether.

Now what? Will the man try to flee, or lunge for the knife to wreak more havoc?

Instead he just sat there on the carpeted floor, drained for the time being of whatever poison had activated him. If security officers and police hadn't eventually shown up to deal with him, he might yet be sitting there with a dazed and stricken look, his head in his hands, contemplating the full extent of this new misery he had brought on himself and another.

* * *

"We ought to kick him in the fucking head," an airport employee was heard to say. By now, I was standing out in the main corridor of the terminal as more people gathered. Someone was being paged on the PA system. The woman with the bright red gash on her hand was being led past us. Her face was flushed; she was sobbing.

Had she come here to catch a flight somewhere, or had she been seeing someone off? Would this forever be her memory of her final hours in Canada? Did she know the name of the man in the navy blue windbreaker who attacked her with the kitchen knife? Would she ever again be relaxed and at ease in an airport?

Just as surprising as the way so many strangers responded to her cry for help was the suddenness with which we all reverted to strangers that evening. It was as though the incident had been a brief awakening from a lifelong dream of order and uninvolvement, and we were gratefully closing our eyes again.

(July 21, 1990)

6.

ADVANCED SOCIOLOGY

THE LURE OF THE BRAZIER

Why do men barbecue?

It's a question that has bedeviled philosophers, sociologists and a handful of inquisitive men for generations. In some ways, it's an even more difficult question than the one I've also been hearing frequently in recent years: Why do women make beds?

I was deprived of a barbecuing role model in my youth. Nevertheless, when I reached the age of reason (on or about my 22nd birthday) I began to barbecue, as though the art of charring pieces of meat over a fire were encoded in the very filament of my Y chromosome.

My earliest barbecuing memory is of the time my brother and I were invited by our next-door neighbours on a weekend camping trip to a park near Temagami. I don't recall who did the barbecuing on that trip, though I'm willing to wager it was Mr. Boissoneault.

What I do recall – in fact probably the only reason I remember that camping trip at all – is my brother scandalizing everyone by putting peanut butter on his hot dogs. I don't believe we were invited on any subsequent trips by our neighbours, but today my brother nervously lords over a gas barbecue in his Toronto backyard, as though his past peanut butter aberration made no difference at all.

When I was in my late teens, my mother purchased one of those round barbecues on a rickety tripod, which I assembled in a mere matter of days. For her inaugural meal, my mother bought a couple of pounds of ground round beef to convert into hamburger patties.

I don't think I'll ever forget the mixture of maternal distress and pure helplessness with which she watched most of her hard-won ground round crumble and cave in between the bars of the grill to the coals, which were not quite white-hot but more than capable of incinerating meat at point-blank range.

"There's not enough fat in the ground round to hold the patties together," I observed.

"How do you know?" my mother said, though not unkindly.

I thought about that. The knowledge must have been in my genes.

When you get right down to it there is something brutish – i.e., manly – about barbecuing. It harks back to those countless generations of proto-humans who killed and roasted rodents and other catchable small animals in the African veldt of prehistoric times.

Perhaps the proto-women were too busy turning the rodent hides into gloves and stoles to cook the meat, therefore the job was delegated to proto-men.

A slab of sirloin steak on a grill suspended over a bed of hot coals is not all that removed from a scrawny rodent carcass cooking on a stick all those unimaginable years ago. But it doesn't help answer the question why men barbecue these many generations later. I'm not even sure my nasty, brutish and short male ancestors did any cooking back then.

In my impish, impatient, impetuous youth, when the "boys" and I seasoned meat as darkness fell and the beer supply dwindled, the coals were perfect for grilling long after we'd finished eating.

I say this by way of illustration that neither I nor any of the "boys" possessed instinctive barbecuing talents. It was just a traditional sex role that had been foisted upon us, like taking out the garbage, not crying and punching each other in the shoulder as a token of affection.

* * *

A few years ago, when I owned one of those horrifying propane barbecues – I still have nightmares about that infernal machine – my wife occasionally condescended to barbecue. Perhaps this was because gas barbecues had actual controls, not unlike a range.

But when we left gas-barbecuing behind for the simpler joys of the traditional charcoal barbecue, my wife immediately abandoned the job. Many's the time I've slaved over the hot coals, breathing deep the carcinogenic smoke, and said to myself as the wieners on the grill broke out in unsightly blisters, "This can't be healthy."

And yet men barbecue – men who would never dream of making roast beef, mashed potatoes and Yorkshire pudding on a Sunday in mid-winter. (A former colleague barbecued all year 'round in his garage, but he's the exception that proves the rule.)

These same men who wear dumb aprons with dumb sayings on them and happily flip charred 'shrivelled hamburger patties onto the plates of friends and relatives would never walk into the kitchen, see their wife vigorously mixing the ingredients for Apple Brown Betty or some other effete desert and say, "Stand back, Marge, I'll take over from here."

It's not that I mind barbecuing, or that I wish somebody else would take over the duties in my backyard. I don't even mind it overly when everybody wants their steak done slightly differently, or when my daughter doesn't want yucky onions on her patties, or when the wind is dead and the coals won't heat up properly, or when there's too much wind and the coals are white-hot in a matter of seconds, or when the fire-starter fluid ignites with a WHOMP! and burns off my eyebrows.

The only thing I mind is having been assigned the job at birth.

(June 9, 1990)

THE IDEAL MAN IS A WOMAN

That mythical 60-year old Swede, the man with a face like Max von Sydow and a body like Mats Naslund, is getting more virile by the minute. If you're in Goteborg and an old man kicks sand in your face, your best strategy is thank him for thinking of you.

Swedes aren't just more vital and living longer than ever, they're also holding onto their original teeth at an alarming rate. Of Swedes born in 1901, 52 per cent had lost all their teeth by age 70. Of Swedes born in 1911, only 33 per cent didn't have their teeth by age 70. (If you've noticed a gradual increase in the number of Canadian oral surgeons with Swedish-sounding names, now you know why.)

Swedish life expectancy has been upgraded constantly in recent years. It now stands at 86 for women and 84 for men. The Canadian figures, as of 1983, were roughly 80 years for women and 70 years for men. Hence the average male Swede lives 20 per cent longer than the average male Canadian.

Perhaps the fact that they are living longer explains the characteristic dourness of the Swedes. You'd be dour, too, if you had to endure so many winters on the cold, dark, limitless steppe, with only a stack of Ingmar Bergman videos to keep your spirits up.

The point of all those seemingly endless stories about virile Swedes in their 60's taking outdoor steam baths bare-naked in the dead of January is to make Canadian men feel inadequate and unmasculine in comparison, and to goad us into doing something about our comparatively lamentable physical state.

It won't work anymore.

The fact is Swedish men have paid a high price for their legendary virility. According to Stig Ahs, chairman of a government committee that looked into sex roles, the traditional male stereotype of the Swedish male tends to make them feel "emotionally castrated", which doesn't sound like any fun at all.

Consider: The Swedish government offers both mother and father close to a full year of parental leave at public expense, to be taken one at a time by each parent, married or not. But a recent study found that 80 per cent of fathers eligible for the leave *went right on working* and the remaining 20 per cent took an average of only 47 days off. In Sweden, real men don't take leave.

And yet, says Mr. Ahs, "warm, skin-close child-caring could make men open up emotionally and give them a safety net of intimate relations as a backup in a personal crisis." In other words: drop the Viking act and change the baby's diapers; you'll be a better person for it.

The mythical Swede may no longer pose such a great threat to the self-esteem of Canadian men, but we're not off the hook. Far from it. Canadian men looking for a role model of longevity and relative physical stamina with which to make themselves feel frail and flaccid by comparison needn't search very far. A woman – just about any woman – fits the bill quite nicely.

At the beginning of the 20th century, a female was expected to outlive a male by roughly two years. In Canada, that gap has now been stretched to a full decade.

Though more males are conceived and born than females, males are more likely to die in the womb, at birth, or shortly thereafter.

Males are more likely to become the victims of genetic disorders such as haemophilia. They are also more susceptible to infections.

Males are twice as likely to die of heart disease and 1.5 times as likely to die of cancer as females.

A male's chances of recovery from infections and degenerative diseases are generally poorer than a female's, regardless of at what stage the disorder is identified.

Although men visit their doctor less frequently than women, the diseases they contract tend to kill them more efficiently.

The mythical Swede has dropped out of the race to spend quality time with his children and generally get in touch with his emotions. The role model of virility currently breathing down your neck likes to look good even when she sweats. Fellow members of the weaker sex, say hello to Superperson.

(May 28, 1986)

VIEW FROM THE TOP MINUS ONE

Last week I had occasion to spend a few night in a suite on the 22nd floor of a downtown Toronto hotel. From up there, the wail of police and ambulance sirens wafting through the window sounded like the muted cries of someone trying hard to stifle his or her distress.

Officially I was staying on the 22nd floor of the hotel. Actually, though, I was on the 21st. The owners of the hotel, like the owners of most high-rise buildings in this hemisphere, simply decided to ignore the existence of the 13th floor. For all intents and purposes, the floor directly above the 12th floor, at least in the memory banks of the hotel computer and on the little illuminated squares in the elevator, is the 14th floor.

This fear of the number 13 is one of the most visible proofs that our rational, scientific, bureaucratic age still has one foot planted in the murky superstitions of the Dark Ages. We're capable of flying to the moon, but heaven forbid a black cat should cross our path en route.

Instead of trying to deal rationally with an ancient superstition, we've simply tried to erase our awareness of it. No one is supposed to notice or ponder the implications of the absence of the number 13 on the little elevator squares. Being a trained journalist, I did notice and I do ponder.

In some ways, I find the arbitrary absence of a 13th floor more unsettling than the prospect of actually having to spend a night or two on such a floor.

What bothers me the most about the absence of the number 13 from the floors of high-rise buildings is that it's an utterly ineffective strategy, roughly as useful as that of the proverbial ostrich with its proverbial head buried in the proverbial sand.

We may think that by eliminating the officially-designated 13th floor from our buildings the buildings no longer possess a 13th floor. That view is not only wrong-headed, it potentially jeopardizes the emotional well-being of superstitious people who are staying on the 14th floor of the hotel.

What could happen to people on the 14th floor at any point during their stay is the sudden realization that they in fact are on the building's 13th floor. This could trigger a powerful sensation of panic, particularly if the realization coincides with the sound of automatic gunfire in the hall or wisps of acrid smoke under the door.

Were this hypothetical person to sue the hotel management for not properly warning him that he was actually staying on the unlucky 13th floor, the hotel management's battalion of lawyers would of course argue that the hotel does not have a 13th floor.

It would then be up to the judge to decide, once and for all, which is more reliable: physical reality or wild superstitions.

I've thought of a way the operators of high-rise hotels and other tall buildings could improve on the hollow strategy of "eliminating" the 13th floor from their official records.

Instead of that useless gimmick, they could courageously acknowledge the existence of a 13th floor, and reward hotel guests or people who have the guts to lease office space on that floor by offering them discounts.

As an additional promotional initiative, hotels could offer free overnight accommodation to any persons willing to stay on the 13th floor on a Friday the 13th, provided they've booked the room for a minimum of three nights. (The three-night-stay provision would effectively discourage vagrants who might otherwise take their chances with the number 13 in exchange for a roof over their head.)

Such a strategy would eliminate the need to arbitrarily "remove" the 13th floor from buildings, and would also appease the gods of bad luck who are probably infuriated by our feeble attempts to shortchange them.

(September 21, 1991)

AN IGNORAMUS IN THE AGE OF INFORMATION

A computer-manufacturing company in Minesota has developed a new model that will work 170,000 times faster than the best home computer. This should come as a great relief to all those people whose byzantine family budget was beginning to tax the computing capability of mere Macintoshes and Commodore 64s.

By the middle of next year, the new computer from ETA Systems Inc. will be able to process more than 10 billion calculations per second, yet it will be small enough that its main components will fit inside a briefcase.

The ability to handle 10 billion calculations per second should satisfy even the most financially convoluted household, let alone these computer owners who use the machines primarily to store recipes for spaghetti sauce and the addresses of long-lost aunts and uncles.

In fact, the ability to handle 10 billion calculations per second should put ETA's new computer right up alongside the human brain on the list of Grossly Under-Utilized Marvels of Engineering.

* * *

I don't know if it was sheer stubbornness, fear of the future, suspicion of technology, concern for the privacy of individuals, sorrow at the demise of the old math, anger at the increased mechanization of society or alarm at my lack of disposable income that kept me from jumping on the personal computer bandwagon years ago.

"What are you going to do with the thing?" I invariably asked friends and relatives who, like lemmings drawn by a force more grave than gravity itself, were snapping up PCs left and right.

The answers were monotonously alike: They were going to itemize their power-tools, alphabetize their linen closet, systematize their pots and pans, prioritize their household projects and aggrandize their self-esteem by becoming computer-literate.

They were going to enrol the fetus of their child in computer camp so that the child would come to accept the dull green glow of a cathode ray tube as a surrogate nightlight. If little Balthazar hadn't familiarized himself with PCs by the day of his birth, they'd have failed in their role as parents to prepare him for the increasingly competitive world out there.

What they were doing with the thing was interfacing with the Joneses.

* * *

The best computers, like the nicest people, are user-friendly. The one I'm storing this column on is extremely user-friendly, in that I use it every day for work and yet I haven't got the foggiest notion– nor do I care, really – how many calculations it can do per second.

I feel roughly the same way about my toaster, the lawn mower, the toilet, the car, and so on.

I don't want to give the impression I'm flaunting my ignorance of how certain technological artifacts work, but I guess that's exactly what I'm doing. I suppose it's another reason I've deliberately stayed off the personal-computer bandwagon. Selective ignorance, particularly in this Age of Information, has a certain retrograde chic.

In fact, I am a Yippie – a Young Ignorant Person – and I believe I am not alone. (In case you're wondering, "young" becomes a more relative word with each year the baby-boom generation grows older.) I believe there are hundreds of thousands of closet Yippies out there just waiting for someone with the courage of his or her uncertainties to speak on their behalf. It's only a matter of time before the business world is forced to factor the Yippie into their market research.

There's a great bloc of people out there who are hungry for a return to a more low-tech scale of values – people for whom a pad and pencil are infinitely more exciting than a screen and keyboard; people who use a hammer and screwdriver to drill holes in things; people who wouldn't know a floppy disc from a sloppy joe; people who think hardware is the hammer and screwdriver they use to drill holes.

It's time for us to stand up and be counted – manually.

(June 25, 1988)

THE COMPLICATED THRILL OF VICTORY

Even if I were a gifted athlete -- which I most certainly am not -- I would never be able to compete in any sport at the professional level. That's because I would never in an old man's lifetime master the complex sequence of physical manoeuvres with which modern athletes congratulate one another.

Autumn is a good time of year to see what I mean. Turn on your TV and you can catch just about every pro sport, from hockey and baseball to football and soccer. Forget the actual play. Instead, watch carefully the way the athletes behave after one of them has done something wonderful, such as score.

The most common congratulatory gesture in sport these days is called the "high five". It involves athletes raising their arms above their head and performing a kind of patty-cake handslap with arms fully extended and great teethy grins on their faces.

The "high five" began, I suppose, as an extrapolation of the sober handshake with which businessmen and lawyers seal contracts and other agreements. But probably it's closer on the evolutionary scale to the palm slap -- the "gimme five" -- which is itself an urban variation on the aforementioned handshake. (And you thought this was a simple subject.)

Don't fool yourself into thinking you can get the hang of the "high five" in a few short minutes. There are more variations on this gesture than you can shake a lacrosse stick at. Here are just a few:

- Some athletes slap each other's hands and leave it at that.
- Some athletes -- particularly baseball players -- actually interlock their fingers as they perform the salute. One of them must then decide when is the appropriate time to let go and saunter back to the dugout.
- Some players opt for the "low five", a kind of conscious repudiation of the "high five". The "low five" involves slapping each other's palms, but at calf level.
- Relief pitchers prefer a sober handshake from teammates after they've saved the game. Not for them the more dangerous slapping hijinks.

The reason I can't play organized sport at any level is that I would be too busy sorting out the various elaborate congratulatory gestures to concentrate on that part of the game that supposedly earns one the right to give and receive those gestures in the first place.

* * *

Hockey players wear those cumbersome gloves that prevent them from engaging in intricate hand-and-finger salutes after they or one of their teammates have done something valiant. So they do other things.

They hug each other an awful lot, quite unabashedly. (Watch a game if you don't believe me.) And -- even more poignant -- they go through the motion of tousling one another's hair, even though they're all wearing helmets to protect their skulls from less affectionate gestures.

Hockey players customarily greet their goalie by taking a swing at his pads with their hockey sticks. When a member of an opposing team does the same thing, the goalie retaliates by swinging his larger, heavier stick. Go figure.

Professional football players sometimes gather in the end zone after a touchdown and perform a ritualistic victory dance. Others are content to slam the football onto the artificial turf. After this, the player who actually scored the touchdown trots to the sidelines, removes his helmet, flashes the number 1 with his right finger and mouths a toothless "Hi, Mom" to the nearest TV camera.

When tennis players finally win one of their interminable matches, they usually fall to their knees and thank the gods in heaven.

Soccer players like to run around the field giving each other piggy-back rides after a goal. Can you blame them? They score so rarely in that brutally ungratifying sport.

A golfer tips his hat to the gallery after sinking a long and difficult putt. He saves the high-fives and the piggy-back rides for later, with his wife.

* * *

It has become customary, upon completion of the World Series, for the catcher of the winning team to jump into the arms of his pitcher, and for everyone else on the club to pile on top of those two.

In the average workaday office, the catharsis is somewhat more subdued. If a particular company has had a winning season, a memo may circulate to that effect. Or a couple of extra bucks may find their way into the employee's pay envelope.

Somehow, this seems less satisfying than all the jumping around and complex slap manoeuvres of professional sport. So does the salary level, but that's another column.

(September 9, 1987)

NOTHING EXCEEDS LIKE EXCESS

Perhaps it's because of the daily diminution of available light as the planet's calendar approaches the winter solstice.

Perhaps it's because of the advent of Christmas, followed by the frenzied "Boxing Week" sales (some retailer inevitably is going to proclaim "Boxing Month" one of these years), and the ensuing New Year's Eve spectacle of saturnalian jollity and merriment.

Whatever the case, December is the month of the year when excessive human behaviour achieves its fullest expression – wherever excess is available, that is.

While the rest of nature in this part of the world settles in for the sleepy consumption of stored nuts and a general retreat from the harsh conditions of winter, we human beings start gearing up.

Sometimes on a still December night, you can hear the grinding of human gears above the sound of tree limbs hardening in the icy air.

* * *

Take procreation:

In December, while most reasonable animals tend to lose their enthusiasm for makin' whoopie – no doubt in an effort to conserve energy against winter – we humans are in the mood like no other month of the year. Fuelled by hot toddies, spiked nogs, turkey, cranberry sauce and fruitcake, we love one another to such a degree that the birth rate in September shoots up a full 10 per cent higher than at its lowest point, in early winter.

I needn't go into much detail about retail sales figures for the month of December compared to the rest of the year. Had the Three Wise Men shopped in today's persuasive commercial market, they would have delivered Black & Decker power tools and a Nintendo video game set to Bethlehem in lieu of myrrh and frankincense – and they would have been on a long waiting list for the Nintendo.

Woe betide those citizens who wander innocently into the main shopping districts of the community to buy a light bulb or a new pair of underwear at this time of year. They'll be carried off by the floes and eddies of a populace becoming more desperately consumptive with the passing of each SDTX (Shopping Day 'Till X-mas).

Subject to the peer pressure of the shopping throng, lulled into complacency by the carols wafting out of the various Muzak systems, laden with unnecessary merchandise, these unsuspecting shoppers will gravitate to the cashier like lambs to the slaughter, proffering a major credit card with a single trembling cloven hoof.

Only after they arrive safely home will they remember that they forgot about the light bulb and the new underwear.

The Christmas season, so full of good cheer and hectic activity, is not only a time for excessive behaviour of all kinds – good, bad and indifferent. It also happens to be one of the most dangerous periods of the year in the home. Figures published recently by *Atlantic Monthly* magazine tell a sobering tale of personal injuries directly caused by the Yule.

If past trends hold, and the Canadian population is factored into the numbers, some 440 North American will be treated in hospital this month for cuts caused by trying to assemble, deploy and dismantle the artificial Christmas tree.

About 330 children under the age of four will swallow Christmas-tree lights,. and a further 880 children can be expected to swallow non-electric ornaments. (None of them will die.)

As many as 5,500 people will be taken to hospital emergency rooms because of accidents involving one or another type of Christmas ornament, from plastic mistletoe to chintzy Jack Frost stencils.

Holly will be ingested by about 2,200 people, who will react to the poison but survive the ordeal.

More than 2,200 unnecessary calls will be made to hospitals and health clinics about poinsettias, which many people believe are poisonous but which in fact are not.

Millions of people, as usual, will eat too much Christmas dinner and will repair directly after the meal to a quiet armchair or couch, to munch on a few assorted nuts and emulate the bears, squirrels and other fur-bearing neighbours who are wisely curled up in the warmest, darkest, safest place they can find.

(December 8, 1988)

THE BOYS OF ETERNAL SUMMER

Thirteen things not quite right about watching a Blue Jays game under the SkyDome roof on a sunny spring afternoon:

1. Early-season baseball is a rite of spring. The spectacle of the ball players slicing the crisp air with a swing of the bat in the on-deck circle is just as important to the spectator as the experience of a spring breeze with a slight remnant of Arctic chill, and a specific shade of azure in the sky.
2. The combination of artificial turf, artificial dirt around the bases and a rubbery artificial foul territory beneath a complex, concave grid of steely, artificial sky leads to the conclusion that, on this day at least, baseball is an artificial indoor sport. It might as well be mid-January outside, for all we know.
3. Room temperature feels nice in a room, but it's hopelessly decadent in a ballpark. If the Ancient Romans had figured out how to do it, they would have put a roof over the Colosseum for all those important Lions-Christians games.
4. The SkyDome is, let's face it, a large can with a partially removable lid; I couldn't help speculating about the aggregate body odour of 40,000 baseball fans in an enclosed, albeit ventilated, space.
5. No one seems able to bunt on the green SkyDome floor. Base-hits bounce happily into the fielder's mitt like those red-white-and-blue rubber balls of yore. Fielding is no longer fielding, it's retrieving.
6. Looming beyond the centre-field bleachers, instead of the blue yonder, is a wall of glass behind which spectators dine while watching the action in the distance. Above them, well-to-do spectators adjust the curtains in the windows of their hotel room. Where is Reggie Jackson to launch a towering home run through one of those windows and into a bowl of minestrone in the restaurant, or the bowl of a bidet in a stylish hotel suite where only blue sky is supposed to be?
7. Pop flies don't stray from their appointed trajectory, buffeted by temperamental spring winds off the lake. Instead, they rise and fall in a perfectly predictable, mechanistic arc that seems to imply God is away on business.

8. Lake Ontario gulls have a lot more spare time on their claws. Perhaps they roost on the SkyDome roof, waiting for it to open, for Dave Winfield and those other murderous boys of summer to chase them off the strange grass that tastes suspiciously like styrofoam.
9. The Jumbotron, the tallest free-standing television set in the solar system, deepens the illusion of sitting in the largest free-standing rec room in the galaxy. If SkyDome technicians were to show the entire game on the Jumbotron instead of just the (non-controversial) instant replays, we could sit back and dream we had a converter to flick to another channel between innings.
10. Imagine the movie *Field Of Dreams* if it had been about the romance of playing baseball indoors. Instead of inspiring an Iowa corn farmer, the God of the Game would have sought out one of those discount warehouse retailers and whispered to him in the vastness of all that concrete and steel, "If you renovate it, he will come..."
11. The other morning, while watching a real blue jay disport in our cedar tree, it struck me how inapt the Toronto ball team's name has become now that the team plays so many of its games in this new cage. The Toronto Budgies would be a more suitable designation.
12. On those rare occasions in the past when I graced the seats of Exhibition Stadium with my presence, I was invariably surrounded by drunken louts who responded with hostility and aggression to my polite suggestion that they stop spilling beer on me. Since then, I have always associated attending a Blue Jays game with feelings of physical fear and impending humiliation. At the SkyDome, politeness rules. People excuse themselves if a kernel of popcorn should stray beyond their personal space. Has the pendulum swung too far? Should a few yahoos be put on retainer?
13. Gone is the slow, subtly hypnotic arc of the sun's shadow as it traverses the right-field seats. The light in the SkyDome is as steady as September rain. If it weren't for the digital clock on the scoreboard, you'd swear time had stopped altogether and each inning was interminable, like the Stanley Cup playoffs.

(April 28, 1990)

WAITING FOR AQUARIUS

My wife and I ushered in the 1980s by attending a desultory New Year's Eve party, the highlight of which was a young folk musician's thoroughly dispiriting rendition of "500 Miles". By the stroke of midnight and the start of a new decade, nobody felt like kissing anybody.

In retrospect, that New Year's Eve wake was apt, if not downright prescient. After all, Russian tanks had just rolled into Afghanistan, Ronald Reagan would soon be strolling into the White House, Poland was about to be placed under martial law, and John Lennon was living out the last few months of his life.

To say the '80s got off to a bad start is perhaps the understatement of the decade.

Who would have guessed that the '80s would make us nostalgic for the '70s? Who would have guessed that the '80s would amount to the '50s on cocaine: arch-conservative, arch-materialistic, more frenzied but no less stultifying than the age of Eisenhower?

Cocaine, the chemical addiction of choice in the '80s, lends a temporarily false sense of confidence to people who use it. The '80s was full of temporary false confidence, not to mention superficial bluster. Ronald "America Is Back" Reagan served both as spokesman and mascot of the age. The aftermath of this artificial high in the West was a lot of dashed hopes and, by the final two years of the decade, a vague urge to improve things.

An urge, yes, and in some cases even the will.

* * *

To many, the turning point in the decade and perhaps all of history occurred on Aug. 17, 1987. That day marked the beginning of what New Age mystics believe is a period of planetary cleansing that will last until 1992.

The event on Aug. 17, 1987 was called "harmonic convergence," and at least 144,000 people had to participate in ceremonies marking it in order for it to work properly. A good 750 of the faithful gathered at one of the "sacred" spots on the planet, Niagara Falls. Other favoured locales included the Aztec pyramid of the sun in Mexico, Mounts Fuji and Olympus, and the temple of Delphi in Greece.

The central belief of the harmonic-convergence movement is that Aug. 17, 1987 is the date indicated on the ancient Aztec calendars that marks the end of the last period of universal hell and chaos. As of that day, the galaxy is said to be in harmonic convergence, and the planets of our solar system are in the proper alignment to usher in the actual Age of Aquarius, as opposed to the one that was a hit on Broadway 20 years ago.

All of these cleansing vibes are meant to prepare us for our first contact with extraterrestrial intelligence early in the 21st century.

The man behind the whole idea is Jose Arguelles, who sets it forth in a book called *The Mayan Factor: Path Beyond Technology*.

Sure, his theory is fanciful. But if you were to examine if in light of events of recent months – particularly the incredible stirrings toward freedom and peace in Eastern Europe – it might give you a moment's pause, before you went on to something else.

* * *

If, as it appears, there is a positive international force at work in the world today, what are we to blame it on? Has humanity suddenly become smarter? Or, as the New Agers insist, is the planet finally emerging from a long suicidal period marked by astonishing destruction and equally astonishing technological developments?

In his book, Arguelles argues that Mayan and other North American prophecies speak of a chaotic period between 3113 B.C. and 2012 A.D., at which point extraterrestrials will establish contact with us.

"People will be living a life that has an uncanny resemblance to pre-history," Arguelles predicts, "but will be more telepathically charged" – whatever that means.

Brace yourself for scores of Arguelles and even wilder speculations as the '90s slouch toward the end of both the century and the millennium. If flying saucers haven't actually landed by then, you can bet someone will be proclaiming that they have. After all, hope springs eternal.

Had the guy with the guitar at that party on New Year's Eve 1979 known about the imminent harmonic convergence and alien visitation, he might have chosen something a little more upbeat to ring in the new decade. "Let The Sunshine In", for instance.

(December 30, 1989)

7.

THE BIRDS AND THE BEES

SEX AND THE SINGLE GLADIOLA

This remarkably voluptuous peony blossom droops close to the ground, not far from where my dog likes to leave his scent. Do I let nature take its tragic course, or do I gently snip the flower and carry it into the house where it will fill hundreds of square feet with a fragrance that has more to do with seduction than horticulture?

They say gardening is relaxing. I see gardening as a series of moral dilemmas.

My second problem involves a bunch of bulbs we buried several weeks ago. We've been patiently awaiting the sprouting of an assortment of perennials. All we're getting are what look like the ends of roots poking out of the ground and slowly baking in the sun.

Did we plant the bulbs upside down, for crying out loud? Help me, somebody. Do perennials have enough savvy to right themselves underground, or do they deliberately mock the stupidity of the gardener who plants them that way by blooming three feet under the spot where my dog is most likely to leave his scent?

* * *

At this time of year, a backyard smells an awful lot like a woman. This may seem a sexist statement, but there's no denying that both natural and chemical fragrances are basically sexual in purpose.

Women don't wear perfume to attract bees to help them reproduce, but the motive of a perfume-wearer is not altogether different from that of your average peony: To arouse instinctive reactions.

See what I mean by moral dilemmas?

Dogs and their scents don't fit into this discussion. In fact, any animal that would use its urine as a calling card has a few rungs to climb on the evolutionary ladder before I give it the time of day.

Then again, I should probably sympathize with my dog. His sense of smell is far more developed than mine. All those blossoms are probably taxing the capacity of his modest brain. It could be he's leaving his scent more often than usual these days simply to find his way home through the jungle of competing smells.

* * *

Spring can be disconcerting. For instance, we have an unknown bush that slouches inconspicuously at the side of our backyard. Last week, it exploded in a multitude of yellow-white blossoms that gave off a sustained, almost minty smell. The transformation was awesome, like puberty – except the bush goes through this ripening process every year.

Again we were torn between deflowering a few parts of the bush for the inside of the house, or leaving it in its virgin state, to be admired for what it is. Our urges got the better of us, and the house smelled to high heaven for a few days.

* * *

I remember coming home from work one dismal afternoon last January and being confronted by the unmistakable scent of lily of the valley. It turned out my wife had acquired a new perfume. It was called *Lily of the Valley*. Something about that troubled me. The perfume didn't smell vaguely like lily of the valley, it *was* lily of the valley.

Is it right that a woman should frivolously mimic a scent that has such a practical importance to a flower?

Perfume lore goes at least as far back as the ancient Egyptians, who used it excessively in their religious rites. The Greeks also picked up on it, but it was the Romans -- naturally – who professed its power as an aphrodisiac. Apparently the popularity of perfume declined with the advent of Christianity.

Nowadays, perfume has few religious connotations. Women put it on them before they go to work, before they go shopping, before they go on a date, before they do just about everything they do.

And yet, for all the lascivious splendour of spring fragrances, there is a seasonal scent that I find even more purifying than spring. That season is autumn, when any venture into vegetation gives you an aroma that's nature's equivalent of a sweaty running shoe.

Nothing is headier than rot, the state of a living thing turning into a dead thing for the purpose of fertilizing other living things. Rot is not pretentious, rot promises no more than it can deliver. There's nothing tempting about it. Let's hear it for rot.

* * *

I hold the amputated peony blossom in my hand. I peer into it, sniff deeply from it, am intoxicated by it. I resist the temptation to take a bite out of it.

I am a flower molester. Next year, we pave the yard.

(June 12, 1985)

ANOTHER VALENTINE FOR STELLA

When I was six years old, on or about St. Valentine's Day, I asked a girl named Stella to marry me. I don't recall getting a straight answer from her, which was probably just as well.

Looking back on that first bold romantic gesture of my life, I don't remember what it was about Stella that moved me to pop the question. I have only the vaguest mental photograph of her. She was blonde, and I think she wore glasses. The particulars of her personality are entirely lost to me now.

Maybe Stella had a good sense of humour. Maybe she was bright and vivacious. Maybe she was the only girl in class from whom I felt I had any chance of extracting an affirmative answer to my marriage proposal. Maybe she was near-sighted and charming to me because she mistook me for the boy she actually loved.

I don't remember getting a valentine from Stella that year. It was my first taste of that annually mortifying practice of exchanging valentines in class. Here, for a single day of the year, was an accurate way of quantifying how liked or loved you were by your peers of the opposite sex.

Imagine if the same ritual were practised in the adult workplace. Imagine the networking and lobbying that would go into securing a respectable number of valentines from one's co-workers on the appointed day. Careers, let alone personal self-esteem and a lot of previously healthy marriages, could hang in the balance.

Several days before St. Valentine's Day 1960, I began planning my valentine to Stella. I had ruled out sending one of those chintzy little heart-shaped cardboard cut-outs. I needed more space in which to compose the eloquent love note that would win me Stella's six year-old heart for as long as we both would live.

I had already decided upon the central theme of my valentine to Stella. It would begin with the heart-rending words of a country-and-western song that was popular at the time, "Please Help Me I'm Falling (In Love With You)". The way the singer performed it, he paused after the word "falling" rather than the word "me", which lent a deeper note of desperation and even danger to his plea.

I identified with the singer's sentiment. My affinity for Stella was the first clue the world gave me about why fathers and mothers get together in the first place. When you're a little kid, you tend to assume that your parents have been together since the beginning of time, and for that matter were never children. They materialized into the world full-grown and happily married, for the express purpose of bringing you into it later on.

I had been told stories and seen movies, in which adults, young and old, went through the throes of romantic love, exhilarated one moment and heart-broken the next. My main motive in asking Stella to marry me was the hope of settling the matter early in life and staving off the emotional roller-coaster rides to come. I was a six-year-old pragmatist.

My three older brothers took a morbid interest in my secretive valentine project. They hovered over me as I composed, in the less than elegant scrawl of a first-grader, my love message to Stella.

In block letters I set down:

PLEASE HELP ME I'M FALLING

Then I succumbed to writer's block. My brothers waited silently for me to finish the sentence. I knew in advance what their reaction would be. I rooted through my mind for a meaningful but less revealing alternative to the words "in love".

Finally, in the biggest cop-out of my life up to that point, I scrawled the words

SO LOW

to complete the sentence. My message to Stella, sounding more psychotic than romantic, was, "Please help me I'm falling so low." The message may have neatly summed up the way I was feeling at the time, but it gave Stella little to go on.

A couple of months later, Stella's family moved out of town. I never saw her again. For years I imagined my weird valentine had precipitated the move. Nowadays, I wonder if Stella is as happy in love as I am. I hope she is.

(February 9, 1991)

CAN THIS MARRIAGE BE SAVED?

Question of the week:

How come there are never any rumours to the effect that Prince Charles and Diana, Princess of Wales, are getting along swimmingly?

Supplementary question of the week:

How do you define the concept of "living apart" when you're dealing with a couple who routinely shuttle among several residences, all of which have dozens of bedrooms, self-contained apartments, guest houses, ballrooms and grounds that make Gage Park look like my front yard?

Considering the physical environment in which Charles and Diana move, it's a wonder they ever run into each other. An average family may have a pretty good idea of where they'll gather in the evening to watch television. Not so Chuck and Di.

Charles probably has to jot down a note to his secretarial corps, who then draft a memorandum to Diana's secretarial corps, who receive the note, acknowledge it in writing, then duly inform the Princess Of Wales that the Prince Of Wales will be watching *Dynasty* that evening in the Wellington room, which is accessible on foot in slightly more than 15 minutes by hiking across the east wing of the house and hanging a left at the bust of William the Conqueror.

* * *

Despite the highly exceptional circumstances under which the royals live out their days, we tend to relate to rumours about their personal relationships as though they were ordinary people just like you and me.

Hence the front-page story in the *Spectator* this week, drawn from a front-page story in a London tabloid which alleged that Charles and Diana now shun each other's company, and when they do run into each other, it often results "in a blazing row for all to hear."

I'm trying to imagine Charles, the very picture of civility and overbreeding, involved in a "blazing row". I'm trying to imagine Diana, every inch the demure international socialite, flinging a priceless dish across the room at her husband, and the dish landing some 75 metres short of its intended target owing to the sheer size of the room.

Perhaps the "blazing row" is conducted by proxy: Perhaps Diana's lady-in-waiting has a shouting match with Charles' valet, and everyone feels a whole lot better afterward.

My point is this: If we can't possibly imagine what daily life for Charles and Diana is like when they're getting along, what makes us think we can understand the officious, potentially byzantine form their marital discord might take?

* * *

According to the recent issue of a popular North American tabloid, Sarah, the Duchess of York, recently had a haircut in an effort to save her marriage with Andrew, the Duke of York.

Up to now, a haircut hasn't struck me as an especially effective marriage-saving device. But who knows what difference it might make in a royal household? Perhaps Sarah's new haircut will help Andrew recognize her from among the retinue of aides, servants, friends and hangers-on who accompany Sarah on every last shopping trip, every last working ski-holiday.

Rumours about marital strife in the Sarah-Andrew household(s) have been circulating for months. Lately, Sarah's name has been linked with that of the dashing son of a prominent American oil baron. (The rumour sounds a lot like an episode of *Dallas*, which is probably as good a yardstick of the royal lifestyle as any currently available.)

Frankly though, I'm bored by the saga of Sarah and Andrew. The big story, particularly as the 10th anniversary of their glittering fairytale wedding draws near, is Charles and Diana.

Possibly the best hint of the enormous challenges facing this couple is the news, last week, that Queen Elizabeth is giving Diana a $30-million, 30-bedroom Tudor mansion on 28,000 hectares of countryside in Scotland.

Could this be part of a sinister conspiracy, masterminded at the very top of Britain's royal family, to put as much floor space as possible between Diana and the man who would be king?

(April 20, 1991)

GHOST WRITERS IN THE SKY

I dropped into a stationery store a few weeks ago and was shocked to discover the greeting-card section stuffed with Easter cards.

I've never given an Easter card in my life. I wasn't even aware that Easter was an event that called for the exchange of greeting cards. To the best of my knowledge, I've never received an Easter card. Getting one or two would have been a good tip-off that I was supposed to give them, too.

Actually, I've drifted out of the greeting-card habit in recent years. The last time my wife and I sent out cards in any quantity was at Christmas in 1980, after touring Europe. We decided it would be nice to send cards to all the fine people we met on our travels.

The fact that we didn't get a single card back from overseas rather took the wind out of our sails the following year. We consoled ourselves by rationalizing that everyone in Europe probably had drifted out of the greeting-card habit ahead of us.

And yet, judging by the number and variety of greeting cards on display in that downtown stationary store, Canadians are more card-happy than ever. The store stocks the usual array of birthday, anniversary, get well, graduation, "across the miles" and belated greetings, in styles ranging from sappy, sentimental verse to smart-ass one liners.

But sometime over the past few years, while I had my back turned, the greeting-card industry became almost absurdly specialized. Among the categories of cards available in the store I visited, aside from the traditional ones, were:

pre-commitment
love non-traditional
love traditional
difficult times
love humorous
love cute
birthday/seriously ill
sorry haven't written
fun & love
close relationship

friendly support
sorry
compliment

Is there any need to write a personal letter ever again?

There's something almost vulgar, if you consider it with any honesty, about sending someone a card that contains a message you had absolutely no hand in composing. It's the interpersonal equivalent of the Speech From The Throne, which the governor-general reads but doesn't write and may not even agree with.

Perhaps in response to the aversion of some card buyers to the pre-fabricated sentiment inscribed on so many greeting cards, blank cards have become popular in recent years. These usually consist of a tranquil, "inspirational" photograph of suitably photogenic flora and/or fauna, with plenty of white space inside on which to jot down sentiments of one's own.

Another recent innovation, ostensibly designed to excite jaded cardbuyers, is the card with the tiny gizmo inside that plays snatches of a famous melody -- Beethoven's "Ode To Joy" or the Beatles' "Hey Jude".

I don't want to seem uncharitable, but these electronic cards annoy me even more than the traditional "tra-la-la-la-la, with love etc." cards. The tiny batteries that power them eventually die, thank goodness. But in the meantime, the sound they make is preposterously inhuman -- not unlike the peep of the cash register as it tallies up the money you owe for buying the card in the first place.

* * *

If greeting cards are for people who don't have the time or inclination to compose a greeting or message of their own, and if they're as popular now as they've ever been, that simply raises the value of the one-of-a-kind, handmade card from a loved one.

Children excel at this art. We have a box at home stuffed with elaborate Valentine's, Mother's and Father's Day cards to prove it. Hearts have been cut out with devotion and care, then pasted extravagantly to the rough paper. Messages of love have been scrawled in magic-marker in the unmistakable hand and wording of a real person. Small doilies have been glued to the empty places between the hearts, or bits of cotton batten that represent clouds in a depiction of spring. Flowers have been dried and pressed between sheets of wax paper in an encyclopedia volume, then affixed to the card.

Making our own greeting cards, with our own greetings in them, is an art we lose when we grow up. I suspect it isn't the only art we lose.

(May 4, 1988)

TRUE LOVE: THE LATEST STATISTICS

The people who prepared the most recent statistical study of marriage and divorce in Canada say their findings contradict the prevailing view that marriage is the leading cause of divorce in the country.

Of course, it's worth remembering that statistical studies are the leading cause of prevailing views.

The most up-to-the-minute statistics, prior to this new study, were that 37 per cent of Canadian marriages end in divorce. This percentage was arrived at by comparing the number of divorces and marriages in a given year.

The latest study, by Professor Thomas Burch of the University of Western Ontario, was done by tracking people's family life over a longer period of time. His stunning conclusion is that only 10 to 12 per cent of adult Canadians see their marriages end in divorce.

I say "stunning" because it means, if we are to believe the previous statistical reports, that a tiny number of Canadians have been getting married and divorced over and over again. In the process, this small group of philanderers has thrown everyone's statistical studies out of whack and given us all the prevailing view that it's acceptable -- nay, expected -- that we should tire of our spouses and trade them in for new models.

* * *

None of the statistical studies has ever been able to establish whether the fact that you remain married makes you any happier. Nor can the numbers take into account the growing trend, in this age of self-improvement, toward using one's first marriage as a practice run for one's second marriage, and so on and so forth until one finally gets it right.

But Professor Burch has no reservations about his findings. He declares: "The traditional marriage isn't in as much trouble as the National Enquirer would sometimes make us think." (I thought the National Enquirer was too busy tracking down rumours that Elvis has established contact from the spirit world, but that's another column.)

Numbers have a power that extends far beyond their ability to tell the whole truth. Imagine a front-page story that tells us 89 per cent of the Canadian labour force is currently employed. What a happy story that would be for a change. And it would be true! Eighty-nine per cent of the Canadian work force *is* currently employed.

The new divorce statistics may be a classic case of "you say your glass has been downsized but I say my glass shows negative growth". Then again, maybe not. If it turns out the overwhelming majority of married Canadians truly are staying that way – and perhaps have been for years--we're going to have to find some other reason for the meltdown of the nuclear family.

Or maybe the nuclear family hasn't melted down at all. Maybe that's just another statistical legend. Maybe all those TV situation-comedies of recent years, in which every conceivable variation on the family has been explored for its comic possibilities, have been as unnecessary as they've been unfunny.

* * *

The safest way to handle new statistical reports is to remember that statisticians and economists have replaced meteorologists as the least reliable prophets in the world.

In recent months, economists have found more qualifying adjectives to place in front of 'economic recovery' than the Inuit have words for 'snow'. Similarly, Professor Burch and his study team may eventually find themselves prefacing the results of their study on marriage and divorce with cleverly-veiled disclaimers such as, "there's a possibility we've got this thing all wrong."

After all, the old statistics Professor Burch claims to be refuting were accepted as gospel up until a few days ago. Young people lurched into adulthood fully expecting to spend the next few decades trying on several spouses for size. People fell out of the habit of having children because they thought it was inconsiderate not to bring them up afterward. Club Med was invented. Singles bars proliferated. Companions ads multiplied. People dreamed up "contemporary" wedding vows that bound them to love each other as long as there was a percentage in it ...

Somebody owes an awful lot of people an apology.

(March 27, 1985)

WEDDING THERAPY

I'm a sucker for weddings, not because they provide an acceptable excuse to cry in public (I've never cried at a wedding, not even my own) but because it's always a thrill to watch a man and woman jointly launch themselves into uncharted waters.

Whereas christenings, first communions, confirmations and other ceremonial rites of passage often feel trumped up or at the very least contrived, a wedding is a genuine Occasion.

I sometimes think it would be good for us all if we could attend one wedding per week, moving through the various religious denominations and personal backgrounds of the bride and groom, like diners at a salad bar. There is spiritual nourishment to be had at a wedding, regardless of how familiar one is with the people being wed.

For me, the peculiar combination of daylight filtered through stained glass, the snow-white wedding gown and the impersonal formality of the groom's rented clothes works as a pacifier. I could sit for hours and happily watch nervous couples exchange spoken vows – a ritual more evocative, yet less tangible, than signing on a dotted line.

The last wedding I had the privilege of attending, earlier this month, was a traditional Italian affair. The priest who performed the service seemed to know both families very well.

Toward the end of the Mass, the priest pleasantly but firmly asked that no confetti be thrown either in the church or outside the building. He explained that to do so would have struck the church custodian as environmentally harmful. Everybody complied with his wish.

At the reception hall, amateur tenors strode up to the microphone during dinner and spontaneously serenaded the bride and groom. The dinner, all seven courses of it, was grandiose to say the least. I foolishly gorged myself on the delicious pasta, unmindful of the four other courses to come.

I've decided the reason people dance so avidly at Italian weddings is that it's the only way to burn off all that food. Without the dancing, everyone would pass out from their mealtime exertions.

My wife and I attempted a polka of sorts until vertigo and breathlessness set in. We retired to our table, from where we watched the bride, radiant even by the usual bridal standards, float from table to table. (Having once been a groom, I'm realistic enough to know the bride is the main attraction. If the groom were the main attraction, he'd be the one parading up the aisle in church.)

The bottom line – in fact, the only line – was that everybody was having a glorious time.

Funny thing, weddings. My own was a lot of fun, but nowadays I barely can bring myself to watch the video my brother kindly made of it. It's as though the wedding reveals more about how youthfully schmaltzy we were back then than I care to remember.

We engineered the whole wedding. We even wrote our own vows, which sound slightly equivocal to me now, as though we were sentimental lawyers.

The bride definitely was radiant: Watching her is one of the few parts of our wedding video I still enjoy. The groom thought he was calm as a prairie stream until he went to sign the register and discovered his hand was trembling. This part of the story doesn't show on the video, though.

The reception was at a lodge overlooking Lake Nipissing. The bride and groom danced the Peppermint Twist without any noticeable vertigo. People complimented them on their choice of music, which leaned heavily toward the hits of the '60s. For their honeymoon, the bride and groom went to Europe for the rest of their lives– or at least several months.

Nowadays, when they reminisce about their wedding, they prefer to sift through memories than to screen the video. The best stuff – the ephemeral, intangible stuff like shared hope and common unspoken intentions – is beyond the power of any video camera to capture.

(October 20, 1990)

8.

OUR HOME AND NATIVE LAND

YOU SAW RIGHT THROUGH US

An open letter to high school students in Detroit:

I know some of you are probably despondent over the poor showing you gave in a recent questionnaire on Canadian geography and politics from a University of Western Ontario geography student. I want to put your minds at rest.

First, I believe I speak for all Hamiltonians when I say we didn't take offence that you thought the city of Hamilton was located in southern British Columbia. It's an honest mistake, no doubt caused by frequent references to "Hamilton Mountain" on your national media or in casual schoolyard conversations among your peers.

Most of North America's major mountain ranges are out West. Assuming Hamilton Mountain was out there with them amounted to an educated guess, rather than a mere stab in the dark. Besides, you deserve bonus points for being aware of British Columbia.

Hamilton's Mountain, to further confuse the question, is snow capped much like the western mountains – except only in the wintertime. But the view from the top of it is impressive on a clear day. You can actually see the skyline of Toronto, a city to the south of Hudson Bay.

Your reference to the existence of "Sears Bay" next to Hudson Bay was another honest mistake, perhaps even caused by your over-familiarity with Canada. In several Canadian cities, there's a Sears outlet not far from a Hudson's Bay outlet. In your eagerness to do well on the questionnaire, you may simply have been confusing salt-water bays with major department stores.

I certainly was impressed by your general awareness of the city of Windsor. Cynics may be quick to note that Windsor is right across the river from your hometown of Detroit. But my feeling is that the closer something is to you, the easier it often is to overlook– especially since Windsor lies to the south of Detroit, and every American is taught to look north for Canada.

The Detroit student who theorized that Canada is divided into three parts – Saskatchewan, Halifax and the city of Ontario – at first glance appeared to be an ignorant lummox. In fact, that student wasn't far off the mark, and might even have been making a subtle and erudite joke about the peculiar nature of Canadian geo-politics.

The student's reference to a "city of Ontario" is a particularly skillful poke at the attitude of many Torontonians to the rest of the province of Ontario. A Toronto publicist once asked me if I book a hotel room in Toronto whenever I travel there on assignment for the *Spectator*. I told her it took me roughly 45 minutes to go from my front door in Hamilton to the corner of Yonge and Bloor in Toronto. To her, Hamilton might as well have been in southern B.C. (ha ha).

As for the Saskatchewan and Halifax references in this student's complex view of Canada, they are so sophisticated as to be beyond the range of my modest interpretive skills. Perhaps the student is making a sly comment on Canada's traditional geo-economic reliance on natural resources -- in this case, grain and fisheries.

We Canadians would do well to pore over all of your answers for hidden insights into our national character.

And finally, you were asked to draw a map of Canada showing some of the things you know about the country. One of you drew Canada in the shape of a burrito. Several of you depicted hockey players and igloos on your maps.

Instead of belittling this depiction of life in Canada, Canadians should once and for all fess up to the fact that there *are* hockey players and igloos in Canada. What you Detroit students seem to be saying to us is that we ought to be more proud of our national heritage in general – that we ought to stop and smell the back bacon.

I've asked experts in geography, cartography and abstract art to ponder the burrito-shaped map of Canada over the next few weeks. I'm sure once we correctly solve this particular riddle, we'll be your wiser and even more grateful trading partners.

(June 18, 1988)

CAN I GET A WITNESS?

One of the joys of renewing my Canadian passport every five years, apart from paying for a head-and-shoulders photo in which I invariably look like an international terrorist, is to comb the community for a reputable citizen who is willing to vouch for me in writing.

As anyone who has ever gone through the rigmarole of applying for a passport knows, the federal government is not content that just anybody witness and "guarantee" the various written declarations made in the course of filling out the form.

In fact, the passport office has a highly specific list of people the government feels best represents the qualities of sincerity, uprightness and conformity it admires in its citizens.

If you can get over the sheer hair-pulling stupidity of the government's choice of qualified passport "witnesses," the list does offer insights into the bureaucratic mind-set. By recognizing the various sub-sections of society the government considers most trustworthy, you're in a position to draw some tentative conclusions about the nature and quality of the government itself.

For example, it might interest you to know that accountants are on the list of preferred citizens, whereas the people who most often use the services of accountants -- CEOs, international drug dealers and rock stars -- are not.

The government's list of preferred passport witnesses covers such predictable walks of life as a "Minister of Religion authorized under provincial law to perform marriages" and a "Signing Officer of bank or trust company or full-time manager of credit union."

But it's when the government starts splitting bureaucratic hairs that things get interesting. For example, a mayor is eligible to sign your passport application, whereas a mere alderman is not deemed sufficiently upstanding to vouch for you. A chiropractor is fine, but a masseur is not. A postmaster can witness for you, but a letter carrier cannot.

As you can see, the government's list of qualified witnesses discriminates in favour of people with authority and/or authoritative incomes. But the passport office's pecking order is an esoteric one, otherwise any PhD would be eligible to witness your passport, instead of merely doctors, dentists and veterinarians.

Why, for instance, would a veterinarian be considered more innately trustworthy than a biologist?

In the elaborate instructions accompanying the passport application form, the passport office feels compelled to include a disclaimer to the effect that its list of qualified passport guarantors "is not a recognition or endorsement by the Passport Office of professional status or superior qualifications."

If not, then what the hell is it -- and why is it so exclusive?

Why must I spend precious days of my life scouring entire neighbourhoods for a qualified chiropractor to witness my application if the eligibility list is just the arbitrary whim of an idle bureaucrat stuck in a stuffy office deep in the bowels of officialdom?

It doesn't bother me in the least that journalists--even senior journalists -- do not appear on the passport office's list of preferred guarantors. I tend to subscribe to Groucho Marx's view that I wouldn't want to join any club that would have me as a member.

What does bother me is that the government appears to be complicating the life of all passport applicants for the sheer fun of it.

Why can't an electrician, or the plumber who periodically drains my basement, witness my passport application? Why can't a firefighter, or the gentleman who's been littering my verandah with advertising flyers every Sunday for the last several years?

It might console people who are excluded from the list to know that the passport office feels compelled to point out in writing that the guarantor cannot charge a fee for the service. All citizens, regardless of their station in life, are potential weasels in the eyes of the government.

(October 5, 1990)

THE POISONOUS MOOD OF THE COUNTRY

How do you sabotage an open-faced hot-beef sandwich?

The options are virtually limitless. You can inject small doses of foxglove into an individual's canned peas, marinate the slices of beef in strychnine, deep-fry the potatoes in belladonna oil, thicken the gravy with larkspur, wash the utensils in PCBs, steep the tea bags in Lake Ontario, etc.

Of course, it's not as though Prime Minister Mulroney encounters only hot beef sandwiches as he criss-crosses the country in search of a friendly face. People in some cities and towns substitute Canada's National Meal with more exotic fare such as boiled chicken and cream corn, creamed grass pike with home fries, or even the most easily doctored food by-product of them all, the eternally mutable hot dog wiener.

The issue boils down to a question of trust: Can Mr. Mulroney and his staff trust that the seafood placed before him and Mila Mulroney by their gracious hosts in downtown Joe Batt's Arm, Nfld., is as pristine as it was when it was pulled from an oil slick off the Grand Banks?

These are modern times: Trust, like interest rates, is subject to the buffeting winds of speculation, doubt and self interest. Trust is not something on which you can draw an insurance policy. Trust, for a politician, is only slightly less foolhardy than candour.

For these reasons, a food tester (and his or her backup) travels with the Mulroney party, testing hot beef sandwich after hot beef sandwich from sea to shining sea, cheerfully confirming again and again that the Prime Minister has every reason to trust the good intentions of his fellow Canadians.

One of the Prime Minister's food testers was observed scrutinizing the lobster dishes in the Inkerman, N.B. kitchen facility where Mr. Mulroney was scheduled to speak and dine earlier this month. (Given the widespread mussel-quahog panic down East in recent years, it's a wonder a battalion of testers wasn't dispatched from Ottawa for the Prime Minsiter's recent visit.)

Mr. Mulroney's handlers have assured us that the presence of a food tester, on the advice of the RCMP, has nothing to do with the PM's subterranean standing in recent nationwide opinion polls.

What, then, has the presence of a food tester to do with? Are the opinion poll results merely the latest justification of a much deeper-seated paranoia Mr. Mulroney has been nursing since birth?

Former Prime Minister Pierre Trudeau's strategy in the face of almost universal disapproval was much more nonchalant than Mr. Mulroney's expensive use of food testers: Mr. Trudeau thumbed his nose and/or brandished his finger at the more vocal critics. "Let them eat hot-beef sandwiches," was the flavour of his typical rejoinder.

I don't know if Mr. Trudeau ever made use of food testers during his tenure at 24 Sussex Drive. Somehow, though, I doubt the former Mrs. Trudeau, given some of her personal habits at the time, would have been all that keen on having any more RCMP officers than was absolutely necessary loitering about her home at all hours.

The extent of Mr. Mulroney's fall from public grace was put into high relief the other day, when someone on the radio pointed out that a greater percentage of Canadians believe Elvis is alive than that the Prime Minister is doing an acceptable job.

Still and all, Mr. Mulroney has little to fear from the citizens of Canada. Our national temperament, like lukewarm tea, is steeped in centuries of parliamentary democracy. It's not our style to poison or otherwise disable political leaders of whom we no longer approve. Instead, we loathe the leader silently, sullenly through the long northern winter of our discontent. We ward off the cold by stoking the hearth with our resentment and disaffection. We picket Parliament Hill on occasion if we are farmers or public servants. But we don't poison hot beef sandwiches.

In the upper Amazon region, aboriginal tribes use an extract from a specific tree to tip their poison blow-gun darts and arrows. The poison paralyses their intended victim.

If the RCMP is truly serious about investigating potential cases of political poisoning, the Amazonian blow-dart scenario sounds a lot more compelling than the hot-beef sandwich theory. Judging by the extent of the paralysis in Ottawa, we could be dealing with a full-blown Amazonian blow-dart conspiracy.

(May 19, 1990)

WHY MOST OF US WANT MORE OF US

One of my classmates in grade 1 kept a list of 16 names in his back pocket. These were his brothers and sisters. Even though families were generally larger than they are now, Arthur and his 16 siblings were cause for amazement in my class.

Arthur said he carried the list around with him to help him remember the names of all his brothers and sisters. I suppose he had learned to recognize their faces, but it's not impossible that a six-year-old would have trouble remembering 16 names – particularly when some of his siblings were probably old enough to be his parents.

Coming from a fairly average (for the times) family of four, I have trouble picturing what a typical day might be like in a household of 19 people. Did they eat their meals in shifts, according to age, sex and appetite? How were bathroom privileges sorted out? Did they rent a bus for family outings on the weekend and in the summer?

Doing the laundry must have weighed heavily on Arthur's mother's mind the night before the day it could no longer be put off.

I grew up in the generation that produced the last batch of large French-Canadian families. Even by then, families of a dozen or more were a rarity. But for decades in French Canada – and especially Quebec – enormous families of a dozen or more had been encouraged and even rewarded by church and state as a means of staving off cultural and linguistic assimilation into English Canada.

Today, by contrast, Quebec has the lowest birth rate in Canada – 1.4 children for every woman of childbearing age. (The national rate is not much higher, really -- 1.67.)

If Arthur were an average six-year old today, he'd be hard-pressed to list 16 cousins, let alone brothers and sisters. By demographic standards, the change in the average family makeup has occurred rather suddenly and shockingly. So it shouldn't come as too much of a surprise that two-thirds of Quebecers surveyed recently said they thought Canada's population should be larger.

After the incessant noise, activity and elbow-jostling of their own crowded childhood, these unprolific Canadian adults are experiencing a vague, nagging loneliness that probably originates in their genes.

Quebec is not alone in sensing there aren't enough people around. Fifty-eight per cent of Canadians polled last month by Southam News said Canada's current population should be between 30 and 40 million. Fifteen per cent felt it should exceed 40 million.

In all, less than a third of the Canadians surveyed felt Canada's current population was ideal.

Perceptions are eternally relative. A Canadian who commutes every workday on the chronically congested 401 is less likely to find the country underpopulated than the Canadian who hitches a ride on the Polar Bear Express from somewhere in the muskeg desert north of Cochrane to reach his office in Moosonee.

Canada's total land mass could easily accommodate 600 million people, but imagine the lineups at the beer store. So what, then, is the ideal population of Canada?

If almost half of Canadians sense there's a shortage of company in this land, could it be that this feeling has little to do with the population of the country?

Could it be that we want there to be more of us around because we long for the long-lost security of sleeping on the bottom of a bunk-bed with our older brother or sister breathing overhead, of having rivals with whom we share blood and parentage, even of having a list of names in our back pocket?

(June 18, 1988)

HOW TO GET YOUR MONEY'S WORTH

I was doing a little home handiwork the other day when I inadvertently hammered the thumb of my right hand. Despite being in considerable pain, I managed to dial the Ottawa telephone number of my local Member of Parliament.

"I just hit my thumb with a hammer," I informed my MP. "I'm not sure if I should put a Band-Aid on it or should I let it breathe. What's your opinion?"

My MP suggested I contact my doctor. I told him it was his advice I was soliciting, not a doctor's. Surely, I said, there was someone in Health & Welfare Canada he could contact to find out exactly how to administer first aid to a hammered thumb.

"Oh and by the way," I said, "I'll be needing you to recommend a colour and pattern of wallpaper for my bathroom, or to contact someone in Supply & Services Canada who could advise me on it. I'm planning to redecorate the bathroom and I want to make sure my colour scheme is sound."

My MP said he was busy but he'd do what he could.

The next day I phoned my MP to tell him about an adult carrier in our neighbourhood who insists on stuffing advertising flyers in the various chinks of my verandah rather than in the mailbox. "I want you to look into this," I said.

My MP asked me what I imagined he could do about it. I told him I would appreciate it if he would check with the people in Environment Canada to see if advertising flyers legally constitute litter. He promised to look into it.

"And could you also drop by my house next Wednesday?" I said. "It's my nephew's birthday and I really think you ought to be there for him."

This was the day before I called him at three in the morning to tell him my cat had just gotten into a scrap with one of the neighbour's cats.

"What are my legal options in this kind of situation?" I asked my MP. "For instance, could I charge the other cat's owner with vicarious aggravated assault?"

The MP sighed and said he'd get back to me.

"Oh, and don't forget Mother's Day this weekend," I said. "My wife likes spring flowers.

* * *

I am being nickled-and-dimed to death by my federal government, so it's only fair that I should nickel-and-dime it back.

Instead of unduly victimizing Canada's major corporations– which have trouble finding where their ends are, let alone making them meet – the government decided to tackle the deficit by skimming more tax money from the tobacco, liquor and gasoline average Canadians buy. There's only one word for this kind of economic policy: "chicken" with a little swear word after it.

Any government that expects to solve its serious long-term debt problems by raising the cost of a package of cigarettes is a government with a nickel-and-dime philosophy of how to run the country. This is not fiscal policy, this is petty theft.

Since the government is making ever more extensive use of my money, I believe I should make ever more extensive use of its time, and strongly urge everyone to follow suit.

* * *

"Why are you calling me?" my MP asked me the day I phoned to tell him of the problems I was having with the carburetor of my car. "Why don't you call a mechanic and leave me alone?"

"Because mechanics charge cash for their services, whereas I'm already paying you a large lump sum of my weekly income, not to mention the various manufacturing and sales taxes and permanent temporary surtaxes the federal system imposes in the mistaken hope I won't recognize them as taxes. The way I figure it, you owe me an awful lot of services."

My MP said he was not a member of the present government, and felt as bad as I did about the Conservatives' chicken---t budget.

"I'm afraid I'm no longer in a financial position to discriminate between Conservative and opposition MPs," I said. "Besides, what guarantee do I have that your party wouldn't draft exactly the same kind of spineless nickel-and-dime tobacco-tax budget the Tories came up with?"

There was silence on the line for a few moments. When my MP finally spoke up, there was no mistaking the resignation in his voice. "Your carburetor," he said, "mixes vaporised fuel with air to produce a combustible mixture that causes the engine to ..."

(May 13, 1989)

TRUE EQUALITY UNDER THE LAW

Getting married in Paris struck me as a somewhat pretentious thing to do, but my cousin's heart was set on it. She met Gabriel there on a summer holiday two years ago. They have since settled in Chatham, Ont., but she thought it would be nicer for Gabriel's folks, who are getting on, if the wedding were held in his hometown.

Besides, my cousin rightly assumed holding the wedding in Paris would give me the perfect excuse to spend a few days in that enchanted city. She and I were inseparable as children, and even though we had fallen out of touch in recent years, she absolutely insisted I be present at her wedding.

The call from Chatham came out of the blue. I didn't know my cousin was living with Gabriel. I didn't even know she had gone to Paris a couple of summers ago and met anyone by that name.

Before accepting the wedding invitation, I told her I would have to contact the Department of External Affairs in Ottawa.

"How come?" she inquired. "Has your passport expired?"

"My passport is fine," I said. "What I need to know is how much of my travelling expenses the government will cover."

The people at External Affairs were not very helpful. My telephone call was shuttled from official to official, with long waits in between. None of them seemed to understand when I told them the reason for my call.

I made a point of repeating to each official that I would not require the use of a limousine in Paris, and there was no need to put me up in the Canadian Embassy there. Two seats on a charter flight from Toronto to Paris and three nights in a comfortable *pension* near the suburb of Levallois-Perret would be fine.

"What would you have us do?" one of the External Affairs officials asked.

"I would have you make the necessary arrangements and advance me the money for the trip," I replied.

"Why would we do that?," he said.

"Because I'm a Canadian citizen travelling abroad to attend a private wedding. Wasn't this precisely what you did for Jeanne Sauvé in June when she wanted to attend her son's wedding in Paris?"

"Jeanne Sauvé is the Governor General of Canada," the official reminded me.

"So what's your point?"

"That's my point," the official said.

"She wasn't on official business when she attended her son's wedding in Paris, was she?"

"No, but..."

"Well, neither am I," I said.

There was a long pause on the other end of the line, after which the official said he would put me through to his immediate supervisor. I made a mental note to forward the bill for this lengthy telephone call to Ottawa when it came.

The long and short of my negotiations, as you have probably divined by now, is that the Department of External Affairs declined to cover my expenses for the trip to my cousin's wedding in Paris.

This despite my personal assurances that, unlike Mrs. Sauvé, I would not be running up a $3,623 overtime bill for supporting staff. Nor would I be bringing alone a retinue of aides and security officers, but only my wife to carry my money around for me.

I also informed the government that I expected to save the lion's share of Mrs. Sauvé's $5,095 limousine bill in Paris by taking taxis and riding the Métro whenever it was feasible. I certainly didn't expect a government aircraft to be at my disposal, as was Mrs. Sauvé's case. And unlike her, I needed hardly any "decorum" to be maintained when I travel abroad.

So what was the problem?

You can imagine my cousin's chagrin when I broke the news to her over the phone. She said it never occurred to her to ask the government to pay for her and Gabriel's trip to Paris. I reluctantly pointed out that since Gabriel was not yet a naturalized citizen, he would probably be ineligible for financial aid of that type.

I told my cousin my fond thoughts would be with her three weeks from today when she marries Gabriel in the autumnal splendour of suburban Paris.

In the meantime, I'm considering launching a civil suit against the federal government for its blatant disregard of my rights and privileges as a Canadian citizen attending a family wedding abroad. I will likely ask Mrs. Sauvé to testify on my behalf.

(September 30, 1989)

9.

FRONTIERS OF HUMAN BEHAVIOUR

THE LUXURY OF SECOND THOUGHTS

There's something especially troubling about the story last week of the two young Americans who were fished out of the Niagara River just short of the Falls.

Imagine two people spending months planning to go over Niagara Falls together in a barrel, actually working up the guts one morning to launch themselves into the river, only to have a change of heart at the last minute.

My concern is that, like all those previous cases of people actually going over the Falls, last week's abortive attempt will spawn copycats – people who want to see how close they can get to the edge of the Falls before chickening out.

In fact, the two Americans' exploit could lead to a whole new field of daredevilry: the retroactive cop-out.

As an example, picture the legendary Babe Ruth at bat, pointing bravely to the outfield bleachers to indicate where he's going to hit the next pitch, then deciding to bunt instead, and getting himself thrown out easily at first base.

What would this have done to his legend?

* * *

I'm not a total stranger to derring-do at Niagara Falls: I once rode The Maid Of The Mist.

The one time I rode The Maid Of The Mist, I made the mistake of standing at the stern of the craft in a great crowd of fellow tourists, all of us clad in those ridiculous canary-yellow raincoats.

When you're standing at the stern of The Maid Of The Mist and it edges ever closer to the Falls, all you can see, hear and feel is water: All around you is a terrifying wall of it. A scant few feet away from you is the boiling surface of the gorge itself.

I couldn't wait for our little pleasure cruise to end, and wished I hadn't signed up in the first place. So I can easily identify with the sentiments of the two young Americans who decided – retroactively – that going over the Falls together in a barrel was not a bright idea.

Anyone who, as a child, had occasion to manfully climb a tree and then boyfully discover it's not as easy to find your way down, can identify with those two abortive adventurers.

That's what worries me: There are probably thousands of us who want to know how far we are capable of pushing a foolhardy stunt before common sense or sheer cowardice (they are often so painfully similar) gets the better of us.

In other words, would I be willing to slip into a barrel and bob gently in the waters upriver of the Falls, if I knew search and rescue personnel and equipment were standing by to save my tail at the last minute?

* * *

I can identify with the two young American's failure of nerve, but I can't condone their tactics.

"We did it because it was there," one of the two would-be daredevils said after he was plucked out of the water by people who are tired of plucking idiots out of the water.

He's wrong, of course. The fact is they *didn't* do it because it was there. That's a whole other ball game.

As far as I know, none of the observations of the ancient philosophers on the question of daredevilry survived the Dark Ages. So we are left to form our own opinions.

After giving it a lot of thought, I've concluded that deciding at the last minute not to go over Niagara Falls is in some ways more foolish and reprehensible than actually going ahead with the stunt. It's the moral equivalent of Lucy forever lifting the football away just as Charlie Brown is about to kick it. Lucy always implicitly promises she'll hold the ball steady, but she never does.

What's to become of this world if we are robbed of another precious certainty – even if it's only the certainty of foolishness? People who made their barrel should lie in it, or get an ordinary job like the rest of us.

As for any future copy-cats who tie up the resources of rescue teams, the fitting punishment for deciding not to go over the Falls should be that you have to go over the Falls.

(October 22, 1986)

RESOLUTIONS YOU CAN KEEP

Close to a full week has transpired since New Year's Day. That means most of us are into that crisis period during which the high expectations of the New Year's resolutions we made clash with the more sober realities of the time in which we're supposed to live up to them.

In other words, New Year's resolutions appear a lot more effortless on New Year's Eve than at any other time of the year.

Over the years in which I've made and broken literally hundreds of resolutions, I've become a student of this fine and hopeful art of self-improvement. I've come to the conclusion that the main reason so many people run afoul of their resolutions so early in the year is that they make them too specific.

For example, if a person resolves to quit smoking at the stroke of midnight on January 1, then finds him or herself lighting up at 12:08 that same morning, it will soon become evident to that person that he or she has contravened both the spirit and the letter of the resolution in question.

A preferable resolution for that person would have been "I think I might just get around to perhaps quitting smoking, or at least cutting down at some point when I have time to think about it in a meaningful way later on."

The latter two resolutions leave some scope for that often-underrated component of human nature: irresolution.

I personally favour New Year's resolutions that have the word "strive" in them. For example, I annually resolve to "strive" to be a better person. This way, even if I fail to totally realize my goal, at least I have the satisfaction of having striven, just as I said I would.

And besides, as I usually tell myself by the month of June, who's to accurately gauge whether or not I am indeed a better person? Perhaps I'm a whole lot better but no one has taken the time to notice. Perhaps I've become so naturally humble and modest that I refuse to dwell selfishly on how humble and modest I've become. Perhaps I wish to avoid the sin of self-satisfaction, and thus pretend I am in fact no better than I was the year before.

One year, I tried to solve the problem altogether by "striving" to be a better person in such a way that the improvement would be apparent to no one. It worked like a charm.

For those who find some of these approaches to New Year's resolutions a tad too metaphysical, a couple of other strategies spring immediately to mind. One of them is to make retroactive resolutions, based on actions and behaviour you have already succeeded in doing.

For example, one of the retroactive New Year's resolutions I made for this year was to visit and pet some barnyard animals. Sure enough, last weekend at the country home of an esteemed *Spectator* colleague, I and several others paid a night-time visit to a barn with a couple of flashlights. After startling the goats and other animals awake, we proceeded to pet them. As soon as I got home that night, I wrote the resolution down and crossed it off the list.

Another retroactive resolution I made was to have a cup of coffee at the lunch counter of the Woolworth's store in downtown Hamilton. Last Saturday, exceeding even my own expectations for the new year, my wife and I did just that. (When my wife asked where the washroom was, she was told by a Woolworth's employee that the key to the washroom had been lost, so no one could use it. I considered calling the fire department to break down the washroom door, but that's another resolution.)

Another way to overcome the despondency that arises from failing to fulfil resolutions is to adopt a few that are either easy to keep or so unorthodox that no one will be watching if you ever get around to living up to them.

For instance, I have resolved to eat more canned peas in the new year, and to educate others about the benefits of this succulent and sanitary food product. Canned peas are an excellent alternative to frozen peas, which to my mind glow an ominous bright green, as though they were grown on the outskirts of Chernobyl.

Furthermore, I intend to invite to my home those friends who, due to unfortunate circumstances in their own homes, are prohibited from eating canned peas of their own, let alone canned potatoes or even HP Sauce.

This will be my crusade this year – more a revolution than a resolution. Why settle for a few half-baked promises to yourself when you can make the world a better place?

(January 6, 1988)

PACK UP ALL YOUR CARES AND WOES

It's February. Half the population of this area is currently thousands of kilometres south of our circulation area, safely out of reading range.

Consequently, I can pass on the news that most of these absent vacationers are not enjoying themselves at all. They're having a rotten time because they went on holiday for all the wrong reasons. *Psychology Today*, a magazine that attempts to inform as well as depress its readership, surveyed 10,000 people on their vacation attitudes and came to a number of informative conclusions.

According to the survey, people carry the same "psychological baggage" with them wherever they go. In other words, if you tend to be miserable at the corner of King and James when it's windy and --17, you'll likely be just as hard to get along with on a Bahamian island when it's breezy and 29.

This knowledge, alone, could save you thousands of dollars in travel expenses in the years to come.

Social psychologist Caril Rubenstein, who analyzed the survey results, summed up why so few people enjoy vacations: "The majority of those who say they enjoy their vacations most are the same people who report they enjoy their work most."

In other words, people who need holidays the least enjoy them the most, and vice versa.

There may be something to that. I'll never forget a 90-minute bus ride I once took in Jamaica, from Montego Bay to Ocho Rios. All the way, a middle-aged man complained loudly to the driver about how hot it was. I later learned he was from New Jersey. I wish I'd told him he could have vacationed in North Dakota, where it wasn't hot at all.

I also remember watching a family of white folks eating pizza with knives and forks at a little seaside greasy spoon. I had this almost overwhelming urge to walk over to their table, pull the utensils out of their hands and tell them to stop acting so North American.

Of course, a lot of people probably felt the same way about me with my Pentax forever around my neck, like some kind of amulet.

The truth is we all have trouble shedding psychological baggage. Ms. Rubenstein notes that workaholics take their briefcases and pocket pagers on vacation with them; health addicts continue to jog, play tennis, or indulge in whatever neurotic athletic fixation they suffer from; and compulsive shoppers go right on shopping compulsively. Their day-to-day routines really don't change at all, even as their skin colour changes.

In fact, says Ms. Rubenstein, people who go south in the winter for the express purpose of changing their skin colour have perhaps the least fun of all, and bring along the most psychological baggage – even when they fly Air Canada, which has a habit of losing baggage of all kinds.

After reading a synopsis of the magazine's survey, I tried to formulate an idea of what a healthy, proper reason for taking a holiday would be. I came to the conclusion that there is no healthy, proper reason.

Perhaps the best that can be made of a bad situation is to expect the worst from a holiday; that way, there won't be any disappointments. Complain about the fact that you have to go on holidays at all. Grumble about how holidays interrupt the flow of your life and angry up your blood. Tell your boss you absolutely refuse to take any holidays this year.

Oddly enough, I enjoy my holidays immensely, regardless of where I'm going. Perhaps what happens is that I take my workaday psychological baggage with me, leave it there, and come home with a pile of holiday psychological baggage.

At Customs, when they ask me if I have anything to declare, I say: "Yes: It feels great to be alive."

(February 4, 1984)

THERE'S ONE BORN EVERY MINUTE

The Russian-born mystic George Ivanovich Gurdjieff developed a system of behaviour whereby persons honed the acuity of their consciousness by way of lengthy and often repetitive physical labour. Call it menial meditation, for lack of a better term.

Gurdjieff's system roughly operated on the theory that if you could withstand the first several hours of fatigue and misery associated with digging a ditch or clearing stumps and boulders from a field, your mind eventually would break through to a higher state of awareness and you would find that you were, if anything, more relaxed and alert than you were when you started the day brimming with dread about all the mindless work ahead of you.

Gurdjieff believed, in fact, that seemingly mindless labour forces you to break out of the physical, intellectual and emotional routine into which you lock yourself in the normal workaday world. (Some might say watching a ball game on TV serves precisely the same purpose, but there were no televised ball games in Gurdjieff's day, so we have no way of knowing for sure.)

All of us have tasks at which we instinctively balk. My personal vision of Hell is of a place where you mask countless door frames and window sills with tape for an eternity, after which you paint rooms for the remainder of forever. I am not about to seek out that kind of interior work as a route to spiritual enlightenment. Nor does scrubbing toilet bowls *ad infinitum* strike me as the route to Nirvana.

Instead, I have latched on to a field of manual endeavour that enriches my soul without the necessity of depleting my body: I nip suckers from tomato plants.

For several years, I have grown tomatoes in a passive greenhouse. I have had to learn not only the manly art of nipping suckers but the godly art of pollinating tomato flowers, since neither wind nor insect is around to get the job done in a greenhouse.

My preferred method of pollination is to "tickle" the tomato blossoms with a gull feather. There are certain times of day and conditions of temperature and relative humidity in which fertilisation is most likely to occur—which goes to show you the miraculous consistency of nature, not to mention the pressure on me as the living instrument of these creatures' procreation.

Conventional gardening wisdom has it that the best way to increase fruit production is by nipping the tomato plants' suckers–those little shoots that sprout from the crook of two branches of the plant. Allowing these shoots to grow takes some of the tomato plant's precious energy and concentration away from the goal of producing choice salad fodder, much in the way human energy and concentration are sapped by such superfluous concerns as blowdrying one's hair and ironing one's clothes.

The purpose of the tomato plant is to produce tomatoes. The purpose of the human being – this human being, at any rate – is to help tomato plants achieve a higher awareness of their own purpose. In short, I am their guru.

Each year, by late June, my attitude toward tomato plants becomes downright evangelical. Strolling by a residential garden in which healthy tomato plants are putting out spring-green shoots of unnecessary suckers (and there's one born every minute, as P.T. Barnum declared in a slightly different context), I have to resist the urge to trespass on the garden and nip these plants where they so obviously need to be nipped.

When you are certain that you know the error of another person's or thing's way, it takes a colossal effort of the will to butt out – especially when the message you want to get across is the perfectly Biblical injunction to be fruitful and multiply.

If, as the Bible contends, human beings have dominion over nature, it is our sacred duty to nip all suckers wherever they manifest themselves. I am not speaking merely of aesthetics in a salad bowl, nor of the ideal decoration atop a perfectly grilled hamburger patty. I am speaking instead of the difference between a tomato plant's life spent in the highest possible awareness of its purpose, and a maladjusted plant that puts out a half-dozen measly fruit before the first frost, having wasted its time growing suckers.

Considering all this and more, I'm surprised Gurdjieff never got around to publishing a book of gardening tips.

(June 24, 1989)

NOTES FROM A VISIT TO THE MOON

The other night I dreamed I went to the moon. It was a cool place with long, luminous evenings. It occurred to me that I should take some notes for a column. Then I woke up, which effectively put an end to what might have been a fine travel piece.

In retrospect, it's probably just as well it was only a dream, because I had a hell of a time finding a pad and pen on the moon. In fact, by the time I found stationery, I was able only to scribble "cool place, luminous evenings" before waking up.

After I woke up, I of course realized evenings on the moon are not all that luminous, since there is no atmosphere in which sunlight can be diffused. In fact, watching a sunset on the moon has about as much sustained drama as switching off a naked 100-watt bulb. The luminous evening I had in mind is more appropriate to Mars, where there is at least an atmosphere of sorts.

Photos of Mars taken by the Viking spacecraft in 1976 showed an evening sky the colour of lobster flesh, and soil that evoked the red clay of Prince Edward Island, where lobsters abound. I remember staring in awe at those photos after they were beamed back to Earth. Mars looked astonishingly terrestrial. The fact that a planet with an average distance from Earth of 48 million miles looked so familiar somehow made the whole universe seem that much more alien.

* * *

Having thought of writing a column about the moon while I was there speaks volumes about my devotion to journalism. It would have been easy for me to say to myself, "Forget about your column. You're on the moon! Enjoy it while you can."

The journalist half of me would have responded: "I *am* enjoying it. I just want to jot down a couple of thoughts for a future column. Two birds with one stone."

The theme of my column about my visit to the moon was going to be ... I don't remember what it was going to be, but I've never let that inhibit me in the past. Themes have a way of congealing in mid-column.

What I wanted to do, most of all, was to give readers a bit of the flavour of the lunar environment. The flavour was not at all as you would imagine. The flavour was that of a northern sky on an evening at the time of the summer solstice – perhaps as seen from the gravel roof of an apartment building.

So much for accuracy in dreams.

I'm not sure why or how I went to the moon in my dream. The people who were already there seemed to be out when I arrived. The rooms I was in showed signs of recent life, and there was a nice sliding door to a kind of rooftop patio from where you could watch the sun set in the damp, dewy environment.

Any child knows there isn't any dew on the moon.

* * *

Most dreams operate on what is called internal logic; they make sense only within their own eccentric context. But the sense they make is infinitely more haunting than the sense your mother wanted you to make when you were young. Maybe that's why we're inclined to forget our dreams from night to night. The nocturnal logic of dreams tends to unravel the meticulous fabric of daytime common sense. This can be unsettling.

For example, the night after I dreamed about the moon, I had a dream that my dog was sitting on the couch, reading a comic book – or at least holding a comic book in a way that gave the impression he was reading it.

The following morning, fresh out of bed, I confronted my dog and said to him, " What do you know that I don't know?"

He broke into a grin and began to pant happily.

One of the more recent theories about why we dream is that it is a way of running scenarios by ourselves, of testing our own reaction to odd situations and sensations. Classical Freudian interpretation of dream imagery (trains poking into dark tunnels, rockets thrusting into the great black void, etc.) has been all but discarded. Too bad; some of it was kind of fun while it lasted.

According to the more prosaic recent theories, it could be that I dreamed about going to the moon, and writing a column about it, simply to test my own reaction to the problem of writing a column about dreaming of going to the moon.

In which case I guess my dream came true.

(July 2, 1986)

ANATOMY OF A TRAFFIC JAM

Inching southward along Highway 400 on a golden Sunday evening, I was afforded the opportunity to watch young vegetables sprout new leaves on the dark eerie plain of the Holland Marsh, such was the extent of the traffic congestion.

People tend to use various organic metaphors when speaking of traffic-related problems. My favourite metaphor – one that I think neatly sums up not only the nature but the quality of the phenomenon – is the term "backed up".

When a voice on the radio tells me the traffic on the 400 is "backed up from Barrie to King City", I create the appropriate mental image of a sophisticated sewer system that, due to human error, is conveying raw sewage in the direction opposite to which it is generally felt raw sewage ought to go.

I picture broadloomed rec rooms awash in sludge, the fumes from which waft through the ductwork to the upper floors of the house. I picture tradespeople shaking their head, then happily wetting the tip of their pencil with their tongue before scratching out a liberal estimate of the repairs on a piece of paper.

I prefer digestive-system metaphors over cardiovascular or respiratory system metaphors to describe traffic mayhem. Like sewer systems that go on the bum, the traffic problem in the Toronto-Hamilton area is fundamentally a human one.

After watching infant heads of cabbage poke through the rich loam of the Holland Marsh, my attention returned to the various causes of traffic problems. Herewith is a tentative guide to a few road hazards:

1. **Morbid curiosity:** Nothing slows down traffic as effectively as the misguided nosiness of motorists as they pass the scene of a recent accident, be it a multi-fatality disaster or an uneventful fender-bender. Most people can't seem to resist slowing down and having a good, long look. Their slow-moving curiosity results in traffic problems far more serious than those caused by the actual accident.
2. **Men over 45 in caps:** I don't know if this peculiar subset of humanity has an umbrella organization yet, but members all drive exactly the same way. They like to ensconce

themselves in the centre lane of a three-lane expressway and proceed, like an immovable object, at a speed of roughly 15 k/h less than the flow of traffic. They don't believe in rearview mirrors and they signal a lane change several kilometres in advance.

3. **Men under 45 in caps:** The characteristics of this group are almost diametrically opposed to those of the men-over-45-in-caps group. (It would be interesting to see if there's any eventual membership overlap between the two camps.) Drivers in this group like the windows open and the cassette deck loud, have had or are about to have muffler problems, like to change two lanes at a time, never signal anything and instinctively tailgate. They're going nowhere in a hurry.
4. **Drivers gesturing at their spouse or significant other:** We've all seen this species of driver. We might even have belonged to the species from time to time. These drivers are so busy arguing a serious and pertinent point with their loved one that they're unaware they've been straddling the centre line for more than a kilometre. They also don't notice as you overtake them and give them a withering look. Hence they don't wither.
5. **The setting sun:** It may seem a picturesque and evocative cosmic phenomenon to some, but to motorists heading in a westerly direction in late afternoon, that big high-beam in the sky causes temporary blindness, slower speeds, shorter fuses and longer travelling time.
6. **Vehicles with flashing lights on their roof:** Be they a Humane Society patrol van or a Ministry of Transportation functionary on a drive to a doughnut shop, be their lights flashing or not, nothing lightens the gas-pedal foot of a motorist more than vehicles with lights on their roof. Encounter one on a stretch of highway in heavy traffic and the brake lights of oncoming traffic will light up in response like a great neon necklace stretching back to your own right foot.
7. **Bumper stickers:** The one that almost caused me to go off the road the first time I saw it was WHOEVER DIES WITH THE MOST TOYS WINS. I've since seen the same

philosophical message countless times. In the hope of deterring a few future sticker buyers, I wish to make it known that I refuse to honk even if I do love Jesus.

(June 3, 1989)

SETTING A PROPER PRECEDENT

The older you get, the harder it is to find things you can do for the very first time.

Most of the activities that don't involve a direct risk to life and limb, like reading the newspaper, have already been tried. Meanwhile, skydiving looms less realistically on one's lifestyle horizon with each passing year.

There are some reasonably passive activities which I have not yet got around to doing, such as riding a horse. This is not because I have any innate fear of horses. It's simply a combination of the fact that an opportunity to ride a horse has rarely presented itself, and I've not been inclined to go out hunting for the opportunity.

Not once have I water-skied or bobbed for an apple. (The two activities are not related, except to the extent that they both involve periodic submersion in water and could result in drowning.)

Never having actually witnessed it in my youth, I had the impression bobbing for apples was a mythical event mythical children participated in on some storybook Halloween night when everybody gets tons of Cadbury bars instead of rancid oranges and stale Rice Krispies squares. The razor-blade-in-apples panic of recent years took some of the mythical glamour out of the custom.

Water-skiing seems aimless and silly to me, like the summertime equivalent of attaching your downhill skis to a snowmobile and letting yourself be drawn through the wintry woods. If water-skiing weren't so intrinsically boring, young show-offs wouldn't have to try to impress us by skiing on one ski, or on their bare feet or bellies – none of which knocks either of my socks off.

* * *

The other evening, my wife and I took our cat for a night drive in the car. This was a first for both ourselves and our cat.

Our cat seemed even more well-behaved and attentive in the car by night than she is by day. She was particularly intrigued by the strobe effect of the passing lights on the Charlton Street underpass east of John Street.

I tried to imagine what our cat must have made of this night drive. She's smart as a whip, but I'm not sure she fully realizes she and we are the ones doing the moving, not the outside world. For her, a night drive is probably the equivalent of that scene in *2001: A Space Odyssey* when the astronaut is propelled through the psychedelic Star Gate and ends up in a brightly-lit suite of Toronto's King Edward Hotel with a big black slab at the foot of his bed (which is a first for the astronaut).

During daytime car rides, our cat breaks into a full-throated meow as she surveys the swiftly passing world. We haven't decided whether this unique meow of hers is meant to communicate pleasure, concern, horror, mystification, unease, discomfort, anticipation, alarm, gratitude, contempt or a subtle combination of all of these.

We have theorized that our cat's "motor vehicle meow" has something to do with the fact that every time we put her in the car, it's to take her to what we euphemistically call Club Limbo, where she is forced to languish in a small cage until such time as we come back from holidays and pick her up.

The recent night drive in the car was meant to reassure her that it's possible to get into the car without landing behind bars.

* * *

Common sense and the laws of physics prevent us from indulging some of our wilder notions about things worth doing a first time. This is probably just as well. But last week's saga of the fellow from Caistor Centre who tried to go over Niagara Falls in a barrel a second time struck me as a textbook case of pushing one's luck.

Doesn't this man know the second time can't be possibly as thrilling or impressive as his inaugural journey down the Falls?

Hasn't he taken into consideration the fact that by trying to survive a second Niagara Falls plunge, he is jeopardizing the potential fulfilment of a lot of future dare-devils who might no longer consider going over Niagara Falls the first time nearly as great an achievement as going over Niagara Falls a second, third or even tenth time.

If at first you succeed, leave well enough alone.

(I think I just coined my first maxim.)

(July 28, 1990)

10.

VACATIONS FROM REALITY

GO SOUTH, YOUNG MAN

"Migration, like reproduction, has a high priority in evolution and therefore, in many species it tends to be confined to definite time slots."

-Jeremy Campbell,
Winston Churchill's Afternoon Nap

Eleven and a half years ago, I travelled to the tropics for the first time. By now, the instinctive urge to continue to do so every winter is roughly equal to that of your average finch.

The first symptoms of the migratory urge surface early in December – right about now, to be exact. At first, the desire to flee to a sunny beach is tempered by the anticipation of Christmas and the various snowy, sentimental winter-wonderland associations Christmas conjures in the collective mind.

But by the start of January, the migratory instinct is unchallenged by any other concern. By mid-January, if I don't go south for a little while, it occurs to me my soul might simply wither away.

My soul won't actually wither away, of course, But there's no talking sense to a human spirit on one of those bitter-mid-January afternoons when credit card invoices come a-calling and the batteries are starting to leak acid into the toys all the children have discarded.

Our very first port of call was Nassau, in the winter of 1978. We stayed in a balcony-less hotel room in the heart of that picturesque Bahamian town, across the street from a stretch of beach, a steady trade wind, a blue-green inlet and a picturesque lighthouse. "Gadzooks!" I said for about the thirtieth time that day, feeling the same way a robin must feel when it makes landfall on the Gulf Coast in late autumn.

The simple truth one discovers upon arriving in the tropics is that, in terms of climate and vegetation, North America barely qualifies as a Third World continent. Not only do we get the short end of the total daylight stick during the winter months; even our summers have trouble comparing with the blend of sun, sea and cooling breezes that are a staple of the Caribbean Islands.

The majority of bird species that are foolhardy enough to mate and nest in northern climes have the good sense to wing it south in the fall. Their migratory urge is triggered by changes in the amount of daytime hours, temperature and food supply. (OK, food supply is not that big an issue with humans who travel south in the winter. But when was the last time you saw breadfruit in Loblaws?)

Like humans, birds gather in flocks before undertaking the arduous southern voyage. Unlike humans, they don't receive a complimentary beach bag.

The all-time champion of migrating birds is the Arctic tern, which sometimes covers more than 35,000 kilometres in its annual travels from pole to pole. (It's interesting to note that blue jays don't migrate at all, whereas the Toronto Blue Jays are annually spotted in Dunedin, Fla. by early February.)

Ornithologists speculate that the migrating urge in birds has been evolving for some 40 million to 50 million years. We humans can't claim such an extensive background in the art. But since our species is said to have been born in the African veldt, who's to say what primal urges to be someplace warm lurk at the base of the cerebral cortex, waiting for the first snow to be activated?

We have much to learn from our bird friends. Even global human demographics parallel long-established patterns in the bird community. For example, the higher incidence of human reproduction in tropical and sub-tropical areas of the planet as opposed to where you and I live is an uncanny reflection of the places where birds do it.

People who make a habit of observing this kind of thing have noted 1,556 species of birds mating in the tropical forest of Colombia, a mere six degrees north of the equator. Meanwhile on Ellesmere Island, the northernmost extremity of Canadian land, only 14 species have been caught in the act.

I'd like to find those 28 birds and urge them to seek professional counselling.

(December 9, 1989)

A WRECKLESS ADVENTURE

The mood aboard the Boeing 737 prior to takeoff from Toronto is one of merriment and enthusiastic chatter – right up until the flight attendants begin their pre-flight safety demonstration. At that point, an eerie silence settles over the cabin.

In the good old days, passengers tended to ignore the attendant's weary-voiced briefing. These days, we're like model students who know we're going to be quizzed after the flight about how to properly deploy the oxygen masks after the cabin loses pressure.

Some passengers actually crane their neck to see where the emergency doors are located as the flight attendants point indifferently to them. Others bend forward to determine exactly where the life preservers are stored under their seat in the event of an "incident" over water.

Fear of flying is more general than ever in this age of structural fatigue and terrorist stamina. Applause is no longer reserved for the completion of the flight. People also applaud successful take-off, intact fuselages, the absence of plastic explosives in the cargo hold, honest-to-goodness metal utensils with the meals, etc.

This lends a whole new flavour of reckless (and with any luck, wreckless) adventure to an otherwise routine charter flight.

* * *

As everyone knows, the first five minutes of a flight are when an "incident" is most likely to occur. The engines are at full thrust, the body of the aircraft is vibrating from this all-out assault on inertia, and it's hard not to speculate on whether there's enough runway to get this great metal beast off the ground.

I had said before we left home that I didn't want to know the plane we were flying was a Boeing. Boeings have had an alarming inclination in recent months to come apart in mid-air. As far as I am concerned, the flight attendants could have dispensed with telling us the brandname of our aircraft.

Later in the flight, as my Walkman feeds the soothing strains of George Frideric Handel into my ears, I wonder if the little cassette machine will continue to play in the event that I, my seat and the beef-like object next to the potato-like object on the plate I am staring at, are sucked out of the aircraft during an "incident".

"Red or white wine, Mr. Rushdie?" some joker sitting behind me is heard to say.

* * *

Turbulence is part of the natural order of things. Recent scientific research has shown that turbulence is a key element in the onset of chaos, which itself is merely a somewhat less orderly manifestation of order in the universe. In other words, just because you lose a few socks in the dryer doesn't mean God is playing dice with the universe.

Our Boeing 737 ascends a bit to avoid the worst turbulence caused by a bank of thunderstorms suspended over Florida. Nevertheless, the aircraft is buffeted and rattled by countless invisible potholes in the sky.

It occurs to me that since Earth hurtles through space around the sun at a speed of 67,750 miles per hour, it's a wonder we can stand on the ground with any degree of ease, let alone fly from Toronto to the Caribbean in a vehicle that is obviously too heavy and ungainly to defy gravity and several other physical laws in such a blatant fashion.

Toward the end of the five-hour flight, the cabin lights on the right side of the plane suddenly shut off. An electrical problem, probably. A few passengers make wisecracks about it. A minor electrical snag, undoubtedly.

Yet a silent question sits heavily, sourly on my tongue: Is the aircraft's landing gear electrically controlled?

San Andres Island is a two-mile by eight-mile strip of land in the western end of the Caribbean sea. It used to belong to the British Empire but now it belongs to Colombia. Our pilot has no apparent difficulty locating it, electrical problems notwithstanding.

Just to be safe, the passengers reserve their applause for after the successful firing of the retrojets that slow the plane after it has touched down. They know that the last five minutes of a flight are the second most dangerous time for "incidents".

But there is no incident. The plane taxies up to the small airport terminal. We take off our socks. Bright, humid air wafts into the cabin after the crew opens the door. We're safe, for now.

(April 22, 1989)

SNAPSHOTS OF A DUTY-FREE PORT

My slide show from a visit to San Andres Island, Colombia:

CLICK: This is me standing on the balcony of our hotel room, gazing incredulously at the bluegreen Caribbean Sea. After several winter months in Canada during which the outdoor colour scheme ranged mainly from slate grey to taupe to black and back to slate again, the sudden profusion of light and primary colours is the visual equivalent of eating a whole chocolate cheesecake in one sitting. (Burp.)

CLICK: This is my wife discovering that I secretly stuffed my favourite Hawaiian shirt into our suitcase. She has a long-standing vendetta against that shirt. I'll have to watch her carefully over the next few days.

CLICK: This is a view of our sunlit breakfast table in the restaurant of the Hotel El Isleno. The hand moving in from the right of the frame belongs to one of the hotel's fastidious waiters who expertly jockey bowls, cups, plates, cutlery and ashtrays around the table as they deliver the best service we've had anywhere in the world, let alone in the characteristically casual West Indes. As yet unaccustomed to the local currency, I hand the waiter a 100-peso tip. He beams with delight. I wonder how much I gave him. It turns out to be roughly 35 Canadian cents. Is the waiter having me on?

CLICK: This was taken inside one of the two casinos in downtown San Andres. The cheerless atmosphere reminds me of a funeral home. The casinos are where tourist dollars come to die. That's us at the blackjack table, presided over by an officious young woman in a tight black dress. The perplexed look on my face arises from the fact that the woman is dealing the cards so fast that she clears the chips away even before we've counted our own losing hand, let alone the six decks of cards from which she's dealing. This is not gambling, this is foreign aid.

CLICK: The man going into the camera store near the restaurant where you can get a steak, potatoes and a salad for $3 is a hotelmate of ours who discovered how much cheaper it is to get his film processed in San Andres than in Canada. As soon as he finishes a roll he rushes over to the store and gets his photos back in an hour. He and his wife are effectively reliving their vacation while having it – a kind of pre-emptive nostalgia.

CLICK: Here's the same man haggling with a clerk in one of the liquor stores. The whole island is a duty-free port. A 40-ounce bottle of Remy Martin cognac sells for roughly $18. The man has just purchased eight 40-ouncers of the cognac. He's trying to convert pesos into dollars on his pocket calculator. He'll worry about the enforcers at Canada Customs later.

CLICK: This is a rear view of a pair of female tourists from mainland Colombia wearing their quaint traditional folk dress: the string bikini. My camera must have gone off by accident.

CLICK: This is us on a short, suicidal speedboat ride from the beach outside our hotel to nearby Johnny Cay. What you see written on my face is naked panic. The man standing casually behind me is the person who is operating the boat. He doesn't understand any English, hence my cries of "I'll kill you if you don't slow this thing down" are lost on him. The boat's prow is ramming into the five-foot swells at a 60-degree angle relative to the horizon. That's why all you can see in this photo are the whites of my eyes and a whole lot of blue sky.

CLICK: This is my wife and I on Johnny Cay after our little speedboat cruise. My wife is having fresh barbecued kingfish for lunch. I'm too worried about the inevitable boat trip back to our hotel to eat anything. Someone is playing Bob Marley and the Wailers so loud it's a wonder you can't see the music in this photo.

CLICK: The palm trees here grow very tall and stately, as you can tell from this picture. Coconuts are the island's main industry. The pina coladas we are sipping from hollowed-out coconuts make a beeline to our already sun-baked synapses. This close to the equator, drinking seems to sober you up.

CLICK: Siesta time. My daughter snapped this splendid candid photo of my wife trying to slip my favourite Hawaiian shirt off me while I snooze. Had she succeeded, she probably would have wrapped the shirt around a heavy stone and given it to the aforementioned speedboat operator to jettison at sea. But she didn't succeed.

CLICK: Here's a beach vendor dangling coral necklaces in my face. "We get all the coral we need in Lake Ontario," I tell him. We haven't bought any Caribbean coral jewelry since a vendor we befriended in Barbados told us he and his associates regularly fly up to Harlem to buy it all.

CLICK: Another accidental photo of sunbathing females from the Latin American mainland. Sorry about that.

CLICK: Our last day. A couple down the beach from us appear to have cracked open a bottle of Mazola Oil to get the most out of their final few hours of self-barbecuing before boarding the plane home. My wife deploys the "Paba 2" suntan lotion. Seventy dollars and a half-dozen grades of suntan lotion later, we've graduated to the stuff with the least sunscreen. I can't describe the feeling of accomplishment.

(April 29, 1989)

SISYPHUS WOULD HAVE UNDERSTOOD

In the interest of historical accuracy and a realistic perspective on the pleasures of life, I like to divide my annual summer holidays into two distinct parts:

There's the holiday itself, an always-pleasurable break from the work and home routine that usually involves leisurely travel to places where thousands of others are doing the same. I think of it as a kind of carnival of leisure: Some attractions are more attractive than others and the candy-floss sticks to your fingers, but it sure beats sitting in traffic on the way to the plant.

And there's the pre-holiday planning, which seems to unfold like some hellish reverse-image of the holiday itself. When I was a child, had I more fully appreciated the number of things that needed to be done in order to do as little as possible, I might have become the Albert Camus of my generation.

Camus wrote a book called *The Myth Of Sisyphus*, drawing on the classical Greek tale of Sisyphus who is sentenced to roll a boulder up a hill, only to have it roll back down again and be forced to roll it back up again, at which point it of course rolls back down again, and so on and on for eternity.

The Greeks were seemingly prone to this kind of depressive imagery. Another mythical character, Prometheus, was fated to have his liver forever devoured by an eagle, all because he stole some fire. Then there's Pygmalion, who sculpted a perfectly wonderful statue of the ideal woman, only to have the thing come to life.

I'm not trying to equate pre-holiday logistics with depressive Greek mythology, but somehow the metaphor fits.

The first priority of pre-holiday planning in our household is garbage disposal. If you don't properly dispose of your garbage before you leave for the cottage or the campground or the capitals of Europe, you'll return to find hundreds and hundreds of maggots in, under and around your bags of garbage.

Maggots are aptly-named tiny beige worms that thrive on decaying organic matter. My daughter tells me they are the larval stage of the housefly, which, as far as I'm concerned, is the ultimate stage of organic uselessness in our solar system.

Houseflies don't have the sense, like their maggot forbearers, to stay close to the garbage and feed on it. Instead, they have to light on the tip of your nose, then buzz off before you can properly dispose of them.

I'm digressing, but that's appropriate. Digression is one of the main hazards of pre-holiday planning. You digress to the hardware store for some maggot-poison because you haven't properly disposed of your garbage before you started planning the vacation. You digress to the drugstore for an antihistamine to counteract the effects on your respiratory system of the stuff you sprayed on the maggots. You digress to the department store for a new suitcase because the one you unwisely stored in the basement has been colonized by a yucky layer of fungus material. You digress to the locksmith to see if he can pry open the new suitcase into which you've accidentally locked they keys. And so forth.

Once you've solved the garbage-disposal and suitcase dilemma, you're ready to move on to pet arrangements.

If you don't happen to have pets, you're missing out on a particularly colourful aspect of the pre-holiday planning. It begins when the pet – especially a dog – has his or her first anxiety attack upon setting eyes on luggage or any circumstantial evidence that his or her masters are about to abandon him or her.

Carrick, our recently-departed sort-of-a-spaniel, liked to play dead right next to the empty luggage as soon as it came down from the attic. He'd just lie there on his side with his four legs pointing accusingly at the suitcases, his sad brown eyes open and unblinking.

Shannon, Carrick's former companion, took a more aggressive approach: As soon as the case was opened, she would sit in it and refuse to budge. She was telling us we weren't going anywhere without her. (Later, when we were about to leave, she'd jump into the car and do the same number all over again.)

Inevitably we did leave, feeling no less heartbroken than she did.

When we returned from our holiday, there was always the prospect of being glared at for the next month or so by the abandoned dog or cat who suffered seemingly endless imprisonment in a kennel so that we could lie without them in a tent in the middle of nowhere.

(August 13, 1988)

BEHIND OUR BURNING DESIRE

Despite increasingly blunt warnings from medical experts in recent years, sunbathing is still a major preoccupation among a lot of people with time on their hands and money to burn – or to tan, if they're careful about it.

Some people see suntanning as little more than a vivid example of the lengths to which someone will go – thousands of miles a this time of year – to indulge their vanity. (I believe the compulsion is more psychologically complicated, but more on that later.)

In fact, with recent studies showing prolonged exposure to the sun's rays can lead to skin cancer or, even worse, unsightly wrinkles, tanning has been proven to be a potentially deadly way of trying to look more alive.

And yet the practice continues.

In fact, numerous Caucasians living in northern climes think nothing of paying substantial sums of money to be airlifted to tropical regions for a week or two, where they can acquire the ultimate status symbol in the peculiar pecking order of sun worship: a winter tan.

When you think about it, a winter tan provides a strange and ephemeral kind of glamour. Upon his or her return north, roughly 95 per cent of the body the tanner has so assiduously roasted in the sun will be hidden under layers of cumbersome, unflattering winter clothing.

And that painstakingly bronzed body, still carrying a hint of coconut or some other exotic fragrance of tanning lotions, oils and unguents, won't likely see the sun's rays again for weeks, by which time it will be as pale and wan as everyone else's.

And yet we tan.

I tan.

You tan (I assume).

Since I don't consider myself much more vain than the next person, I've tried to figure out why I like to lounge in the sun and soak it up.

The image that materializes in my mind's eye is from a TV documentary I once saw about Stockholm, Sweden. The documentary contained a brief shot of a group of Stockholmers swaddled in winter clothes, sitting on parkbenches in the weak winter sun, their faces tilted imploringly to the firmament, as if the sun were the only thing that could possibly recharge their batteries.

It was a supremely touching image, like that of a young flower straining to catch every nourishing, consoling ray from its Great Mother who blazed lovingly down on it from 93 million miles away.

Tanning, it seems, is the vestige of some ancient, more spiritually profound relationship with the sun. The people who worshipped that ball of fire in olden times were crazy like a fox. Modern science is showing us that our relationship with the sun is a lot more fundamental than we might have thought.

Two years ago, the U.S. National Institute Of Mental Health reported that in wintertime, people who were suffering from depression felt better a few days after being exposed to bright lights for up to six hours per day.

In effect, a surrogate sun – generated by electricity – was curing them of their blues.

It was also found that when the lights were kept off, the patients' depression tended to return within four hours.

The Stockholmers in that TV documentary, forced to face a far-north winter in which the daylight hours literally dwindle to nothing by December, were instinctively getting all the psychological nourishment they could from the short days with which they're cursed.

That puts the southern winter vacation in a whole new perspective: What can be more exhilarating in the bleak mid-winter, or more of a restorative, than the gigawatt power of a tropical sun high in an azure sky, its searing heat tempered by a trade wind and the rustling of palm leaves?

The winter tan is just a by-product of a deeper need. We are all solar cells at some elementary level, looking for the spiritual equivalent of photosynthesis. So don't think of suntanning as a mere vanity anymore. Think of it as a sacred mission of sorts – the search for the holy grill.

(February 10, 1988)

YOUR CHOICE OF FLIGHT CREW

Whom would you rather have in the cockpit of a jetliner in which you are crossing the wide, cold, deep, dark, wet Atlantic Ocean?

1. An alert and eager monkey who wants a chance to prove his self-worth.
2. A crew of humans who have nodded off while their aircraft pierces the frigid, inhospitable air six miles above the sea.
3. A pack of wild coyotes.

It's a tough question, admittedly. But it's one that needs answering if we are to ply the skies with unflagging faith in the beings who are doing the plying for us.

That faith was sorely tested with news last week from the United Kingdom that pilots and other crew members on long-haul night flights fairly often fall asleep in mid-air.

One pilot recalls catching 40 winks on a flight, and discovering upon waking that everyone else was snoozing, too. "I had been asleep at least 30 minutes," he said "A sobering thought."

Sobering? SOBERING?! If I were a passenger on that plane, I'd call for the beverage trolley as soon as the flight attendants woke up.

News of the sleeping pilots strikes me as strange, since I never seem to be able to sleep on a plane, even though I have no official duties in it.

One British cargo-plane pilot recalls the time he got some shut-eye over the English Channel and kind of skimmed the water, that's how low his plane was flying. The impact of the water sheared of the right landing gear, which kind of woke him up. He later made a successful emergency landing.

A passenger-airline pilot tells of the time everybody in the cockpit nodded off. What eventually woke them was a speed-warning bell that went off because the aircraft was gradually accelerating on automatic pilot.

"I would think nobody would say this is a satisfactory situation," commented Royal Air Force aviation psychologist Roger Green.

Roger, Roger.

The reason these pilots are falling asleep, according to a team of RAF researchers, is they're overworked and tired from sleepless nights in noisy hotels and long stopovers in crowded airports. (I didn't realize a pilot's life was so much like a passenger's.)

Some pilots have also said the highly automated cockpits in modern aircraft have made their work "unavoidably soporific".

One practical suggestion raised last week was that an audio alarm be installed on the deck of all aircraft. The alarm would automatically go off if a period of two minutes elapsed without any talking or mechanical activity by the crew.

An even more effective idea might be to borrow the audio devices in many late-model North American cars – that faceless man who rudely announces "your door is ajar".

Meanwhile, in Moscow, ground controllers monitoring an experimental satellite mission are having an entirely different kind of problem: One of the two monkeys they sent up in the satellite to study the effects of weightlessness refuses to just sit there and be a monkey.

As well as fiddling with buttons on the satellite's control panel, the over-eager monkey has been horsing around with the electrode cap on its head, Moscow Radio complained last week. (The monkey's capsule returned safely to Earth on Sunday, only a few thousand kilometres off course.)

Think of it: Here's a distant cousin of those sleepy human pilots, stuck in an even more "unavoidably soporific" situation in the vastness of space, and yet he's alert as a pin. There's a lesson in that.

Most embarrassing of all to the Soviets, the monkey was selected for the mission from among 50 simians before being blasted into orbit along with some rats, amphibians, fish and insects.

Picture the rats handing out pillows and blankets to the rest of the happy gang up there in orbit.

Could it be that we're losing our evolutionary edge over the rest of creation?

The third choice in the multiple-choice question at the start of this column – a pack of wild coyotes – may strike you as something of a red herring. But a pack of wild coyotes did devour 48 flamingos at the Los Angeles Zoo last week.

The coyotes got into the flamingos' compound because someone forgot to lock the cage after the zoo had closed for the day.

Someone human, and no doubt sleepy.

(October 14, 1987)

11.

WORLD OF WONDERS

HISTORY CAN GIVE US A HAND

When I first saw the newspaper photo of an immense fist lying at the bottom of the Aegean Sea off the coast of Greece, I wanted desperately to believe it was a piece of the hand of the Colossus of Rhodes.

The Colossus was one of the Seven Wonders of the Ancient World. Like an early version of Mr. Clean, the bronze-covered statue lorded over the harbour entrance to the Greek island of Rhodes, much in the way the canal lift-bridge lords over the entrance to Burlington Bay.

Roughly the size of New York's Statue of Liberty, the Colossus depicted Helios, the Greek sun god. It was destroyed by an earthquake around 225 B.C. – less than 60 years after it was completed. By the seventh century A.D., the last remnants of the statue had been dispersed by Arab conquerors.

Vandalism has always been a problem for archaeologists. Over in Rome, people borrowed blocks of stone from the Colosseum to build their homes and offices. Even the great pyramids of Egypt have been cannibalized over the centuries by marauding bands of sub-contractors.

And if human beings don't wreck things, time will.

I wanted to believe that the giant fist was in fact the hand of the great stone Helios at Rhodes because we can use all the gigantic old monuments we can get our hands on.

Look at what high tides and polluted water are doing to Venice. Look at what air pollution is doing to the great Gothic cathedrals of northern Europe. Look at what modern architects are doing to the Louvre. As for the Roman Colosseum, it may be the most awe-inspiring traffic island on earth, but it's still a traffic island.

What we need are unsullied monuments.

The despoliation of wonderful man-made objects is not new. What was left of the Colossus of Rhodes after the earthquake was sold as scrap metal. Likewise, the Hamilton Drive-In was torn down and a bunch of houses were put up in its place.

This destructive tendency creates an alarming lack of continuity in human history. We can do no more than speculate on whether the Hanging Gardens of Babylon were more impressive than our

Royal Botanical Gardens, or whether the Tower of Babel was indeed the tallest free-standing lack-of-communications tower in antiquity.

Standing in the shadow of the Burlington Skyway the other evening, it occurred to me that some future civilization happening upon the ruins of this giant structure will have a field day speculating on its origin and purpose. Perhaps they'll decide it was a primitive astronomical device, or a religious monument. When you work almost exclusively with ruined things, as archaeologists do, you're forced to rely a lot on hunches.

It's bad apples like Herostratus who ruin things for everyone.

In 356 B.C., Herostratus torched the Temple of Artemis in the city of Ephesus, on the eastern coast of Turkey. This gigantic temple was full of superb works of Greek art.

The temple was painstakingly rebuilt and refilled with art. But then the Goths came calling in 269 A.D. and proceeded to destroy it again. You can imagine how discouraged the Ephesians were by this point in history.

Of the Seven Wonders of the Ancient World – a list compiled by a Greek poet and travel writer named Antipater a little more than 2,000 years ago – only the pyramids are intact, and they've been stripped of all their white surface stones.

All the other wonders – the Colossus, the Temple of Artemis, the Babylonian gardens, the lighthouse of Alexandria, the great statue of Zeus at Olympia, and the Mausoleum of Halicarnassus in Asia Minor – are history.

So a lot of people were understandably excited when word spread last week that the hand of the Colossus of Rhodes had been located. But excitement turned to disappointment a couple of days later when Jorge Papathanasopoulos, the head of Greece's marine archaeological office, said it was just a big piece of rock, of no archaeological value.

In that case, let's do something really constructive. Let's raise it, carve it into the shape of a fist and drop it back into the sea. That'll give future archaeologists something to think about.

(July 15, 1987)

KEEP EVEREST BEAUTIFUL

Forty intrepid British adventurers plan to conquer Mount Everest's garbage this fall. Using metal crushers and portable incinerators, their daunting mission is to clean up the mess previous adventurers left behind.

Why collect the garbage on Mount Everest? Because it's there—all kinds of it.

You might expect the planet's highest peak to be a God-forsaken place where the rare signs of human presence are soon buried under the snow and ice. In fact, judging by the number of Everest expeditions in recent years, the place sounds about as lonely as the parking lot at Lake Louise on a Canada Day weekend.

As many as six expeditions have tackled Everest's 8,848-metre summit each year for the past 30 years. That adds up to a lot of cigarette butts and chocolate bar wrappers. It's inevitable that as trips up the mountain become increasingly routine, Everest loses some of its mystical hold on the public imagination.

These days, aging stand-up comedians who can't find work in the Catskills probably check out the prospects in the Himalayas. Before you know it, someone will build a wooden footpath to the top of the mightiest mountain on earth, with testimonial plaques, informative legends, numerous "Keep Everest Beautiful" garbage cans and a coffee shop at the summit with a sign in a window that says WE WELCOME WELL-BEHAVED SHERPAS.

The governments of Nepal and China, on either side of Everest, officially forbid littering by mountaineers. Among the debris they've noticed on the various routes up the mountain are tents, toilet paper, oxygen bottles, canned food, cardboard boxes, cooking gas, pots and plates, aluminum ladders, plastic bags and the wreckage of an Italian air force helicopter that crashed 15 years ago.

A Nepalese tourism ministry official puts the problem this way: "We tell expedition leaders and our liaison officers before they leave Katmandu for the mountain that the rules require them to clean the mountain. They say they will do it, and when they come back they say that they have." But obviously they haven't.

John Barry, the leader of the upcoming Everest garbage expedition, agrees that Everest climbers "appear to be extremely untidy". Their untidiness can probably be attributed to two factors:

* The intense exhilaration climbers feel when they finally achieve the summit, thereby putting thoughts of garbage out of their mind;
* Fatally injured climbers – and there are still a number of those – are not in a position to pick up after themselves.

One of the most recent Everest casualties was a Canadian mountaineer by the name of Roger Marshall. He died a year ago last month while climbing Everest by himself, without any bottled oxygen. Had he reached the top, he would have been the second solo climber to do so.

"Just me and some drugs for my athsma," Marshall said a couple of months before leaving for Katmandu. "Alone, that way no one else can screw things up."

As the conquest of Everest becomes more commonplace, there's a tendency among climbers to stack the odds even higher. Marshall was at least partially a victim of that tendency: "The goal isn't important," he said before his final expedition. "It's the style you do things in."

And so you have the Japanese fellow who more or less skied down Everest a few years ago. Recently, another Japanese expedition provided the first live TV pictures from the Everest summit. Sooner or later, someone will be the first to conquer Everest in an RV, and so on.

The Sherpas, who've been guiding men and women up the sheer cliff-face to the summit since Edmund Hillary and Tenzing Norgay first topped it in 1953, call Everest the Mother Of The Earth. European climbers have a somewhat less maternal term for the last mile of the climb. They call it the Death Zone. There's probably less garbage there, because only the cream of the world's mountaineers get that far, and they're usually travelling light at that altitude.

Our 40 intrepid garbagepersons plan to concentrate on the Everest base camp, located on a glacier at an altitude of 5,335 metres. Trash is thick in that area. They'll leave the summit, with its unsightly proliferation of national flags, to a more experienced clean-up crew.

On the subject of debris in hard-to-get-at places, a worrisome thought occurs to me: What about the appalling mess the Apollo astronauts left on the moon?

(July 2, 1988)

AN EPIDEMIC OF W-WAVES

Dark tree! still sad when other's grief is fled,
The only constant mourner o'er the dead!

-Lord Byron

I wasn't at all surprised to read last week that a physicist in Oregon believes trees communicate with one another by way of electrical pulses, and actually wail in alarm when they are cut down, destroyed by fire or intoxicated with acid rain.

The reason I wasn't surprised was because of an incident that occurred several years ago, one in which children's sometimes disturbing inclination to brutality was directed toward vegetable entities.

Near the elementary school across the street from where we lived was a small stand of young birch trees. Neighbourhood children liked to play in those mini-woods. Sometimes the children amused themselves with make-believe adventures of chivalry, heroism and selflessness. Sometimes, when they felt less idealistically medieval, they climbed onto the birch striplings and did everthing in their limited power to snap the trunks.

I watched desolately from my living room one afternoon as the children tormented those young trees. After the kids had moved on to less violent recreational pursuits, I wandered across the street and took a tour of the birch grove. The mood among the trees was bleak, to say the least.

The physicist from Oregon calls the electrical impulses "W-waves". I didn't hear or otherwise sense these waves as I did my inspection. But I could positively taste the mood of stoic vegetable resignation in the air.

Stoic resignation is one of the few ways entities that are incapable of locomotion can respond to the injustices of the world, short of inviting tent caterpillars to eat them to death.

The Dutch elm disease epidemic of recent decades probably unleashed the greatest ever concentration of large-scale W-wave activity by a single genus of tree (though there's been a hellish racket in the Brazilian rain forest of late). Hundreds of thousands of elms have perished in North America in the last half-century. It's been a colossal downer for trees from all stalks of life.

The conventional scientific wisdom is that Dutch elm disease was caused by a killer fungus, first detected in Holland, that was brought to North America in a boatload of lumber and subsequently transmitted from tree to tree by bark beetles.

But who's to say part of the alarmingly rapid spread of Dutch elm disease wasn't the arboreal equivalent of behaviour occasionally observed in marine creatures – for example, when whales unaccountably beach themselves in groups and die calmly in the sun? Who's to say the Dutch elm disease epidemic wasn't a W-wave act of solidarity among hundreds of thousands of despondent or diseased trees?

Perhaps the Dutch elm disease epidemic was exacerbated by the sheer unwillingness of a particular species of woodlife to shoulder the burden of being vegetable matter any longer in these despoiled and defoliated times.

I remember when all the stately old elm trees were chain-sawed out of the park at the centre of the town where I grew up. Those enormous trees with their majestic umbrella-shaped crowns provided high-grade dappled shade on summer afternoons. They swayed majestically in a stiff wind and scared youngsters on winter evenings when the bare branches loomed spookily in the silverblue glow of streetlights.

When those elms in the park fell to the workmen with their chainsaws, the park was lost. The park is still there in the centre of town, with its cenotaph, but it's never been the same. With each passing year, more office buildings and parking lots encroach on it.

The American elm was the shade-tree of favour in most North American communities. When you picture in your mind one of those incomparable Gothic arches of green foliage spanning a quiet residential street, you're picturing elm trees.

So much did people love the elm that in some cities that's the only tree they bothered to plant. In 1978-79, some 60,000 elms perished in the city of St. Paul, Minnesota alone. One of the oldest elms in North America, a 350-year-old Great Elm that lived on the McMaster University campus in Hamilton, fell to the Dutch disease in the same decade.

Regardless of whether we accept the idea of W-waves or other forms of vegetable "consciousness", we all miss those noble elm trees. In fact, I'd be surprised if we didn't put out a few unconscious W-waves of our own about it and all the other natural tragedies of our lifetime.

(February 18, 1989)

WONDERS OF CONTEMPORARY ART

The reason so many of us go wrong in our attitude toward art is that we expect art to look nice and to be about something. We don't seem to realize this idea went out of style decades ago.

Today, art needn't look like anything nor be about anything. In fact the smart, contemporary artists go to great lengths to do work that is totally irrelevant to the world around them. This usually ups the price of their pieces.

The simple fact is that the ordinary citizen has lost touch with the meaning and purpose of art in the contemporary world. We walk into trendy galleries expecting nice pictures, witness visual atrocities instead, and leave crestfallen about prospects for the future of civilization.

It's the easiest thing in the world to react with disgust to the recent news that Ottawa's National Gallery of Canada paid $1.8 million – a sizeable portion of its annual acquisition budget – for a large painting by an American that consists of a big red strip on an even bigger blue background. But unless we're in a position to comment with authority and knowledge on the merits of a big red stripe on an even bigger blue background, our objections are groundless. They have to be grounded in some understanding of what art is about these days.

Just because we don't like the idea of paying $1.8 million for a 10 metre high red stripe on an even bigger blue background doesn't mean that the custodians of our tax dollars and the National Gallery of Canada didn't have our best interests at heart. Perhaps the problem is simply that no one has taken the time to explain to us the merits of such a work of art.

Perhaps the two stripes in our new $1.8-million painting symbolize something. There's always that chance – though the title of the piece, *Voice Of Fire*, doesn't exactly ring any bells for me.

Recently the National Gallery of Canada exhibited a series of "Thick Paintings" by Eric Cameron, of Halifax. The paintings consist of several ordinary items – a book of matches, a telephone book, a pair of shoes, a dead mackerel, a head of lettuce – upon which Mr. Cameron applied successive layers of gesso, an opaque liquid usually used to prepare surfaces for painting.

Mr. Cameron reportedly has been putting successive layers of gesso on his objects for about three hours every day of every week for the past 10 or so years – literally thousands of hours in total. In his spare time, he teaches at the Nova Scotia College of Art and Design.

As in the case of the 10-metre, $1.8-million red stripe on a blue background, you and I might scoff at such a project by an apparently knowledgeable and talented artist. You and I might think it's been rather a waste of time on Mr. Cameron's part to "paint" a head of lettuce, a telephone book and various other objects in his Halifax apartment.

That only proves how badly we need the wisdom of a more experienced beholder to guide us into the world of Mr. Cameron's paintings.

That's what art critics are for. They are the important new intermediary in the age-old communication between artist and beholder. Without them, we hardly know enough to know what we like, let alone what art is.

Toronto Globe and Mail art critic John Bentley Mays' recent critique of Mr. Cameron's "Thick Paintings" shed an enormous amount of light on their meaning.

"These inert, mute works seem to exist for no good reason, and to no end at all," Mr. Mays wrote admiringly. "No recent artworks belong more radically to the cultural moment we now inhabit.

"Undergirding his work," Mr. Mays continued, "is a stringent renunciation of the addictions of ideology, action and novelty, and a liberating acceptance of the limits of matter and life, and of our responsibility to guard those limits from violation by the fantasies of this avid, sensual age. Surely there is no more admirable project in contemporary Canadian art."

What Mr. Mays seems to be saying is that Mr. Cameron's paintings are not about anything. Perhaps all radical contemporary art exists to create the need for critics to explain to the rest of us what these works are not about.

It could be argued, though, that if these works didn't exist in the first place, we'd all automatically grasp what they weren't about.

(March 24, 1990)

BLOOD, SWEAT AND LARD

Thor Heyerdahl, the Norwegian explorer, recently talked 20 strong men into moving one of the giant statues on Easter Island. In so doing, Mr. Heyerdahl rather unedermined the argument that only aliens from outer space could have dragged those massive prehistoric statues to their current resting place.

Thus another myth about statues bites the dust.

The previous most recent myth about statues was last month's one about the little statue of the Virgin Mary in Quebec that reportedly bled and shed tears. Chemical study of the Virgin's tears concluded they were made of lard, and the blood belonged to a man named Beauregard.

This news put a quick end to the story. Still, I found it almost just as wondrous that this statue wept tears of lard instead of tears of tears. I asked myself: are we so jaded in this scientific age that tears of lard from a little statue no longer fill us with wonder?

But then Jean-Guy Beauregard, the man who owned the statue, ruined everything by admitting he smeared the statue with lard and some of his blood. He explained that he had been hypnotized by Maurice Girouard, the man who owned the house where the statue was on display.

Mr. Girouard, for his part, had this to say about chemists and other disbelievers: "Modern science would like to destroy everything that is supernatural, would like to prove that the supernatural doesn't exist and that everything can be explained by science."

The local bishop, caught between a grotto and a hard place, originally explained the weeping Virgin as "a phenomenon by which a believer, an exalted mystic who sees supernatural visions everywhere, supports his faith thorough enlightenment from within."

In other words, the bishop wisely hedged his bets until the local chemist stepped into the act and pronounced the whole miracle a hoax.

But where did that leave the Montreal housewife who claimed the lard-shedding shrine helped her son's eczema?

And what does any of this have to do with Thor Heyerdahl and Easter Island?

Mr. Heyerdahl first came to fame in the late 1940s when he organized and led the Kon-Tiki expedition. Setting out from Peru, he and five other adventurers drifted more than 4,000 miles in a boat made of papyrus reeds. What motivated Mr. Heyerdahl was the mysterious fact that the early natives of Easter Island referred to the sun as *Ra*, just like the natives of the Polynesian Islands and citizens of ancient Egypt. What he wanted to know was: How come?

Mr. Heyerdahl hoped, with his papyrus boat trips, to prove that ancient cultures in Africa had contact with other cultures in Central and South America, who then took their culture to places such as Easter Island.

Erich Von Daniken, the Swiss author who sold millions of books in the '70s with his theory that Earth was visited by intelligent aliens from outer space in ancient times, would explain the *Ra* coincidence differently. He would postulate that aliens from outer space visited Egypt, the Polynesian Islands and lonely Easter Island, spreading the word *Ra* to the primitive Earthlings of the time.

The primary evidence for Mr. Von Daniken's theories was that the ancient "Gods" of early myth and legend left massive monuments scattered all over the planet – monuments such as the massive statues of Easter Island, which humans certainly could never have moved on their own. Or so he thought at the time.

Once, in the '70s, when Mr. Von Daniken visited Toronto, a disbeliever challenged his peculiar theology. The disbeliever asked: "How did an astronaut get the Virgin Mary pregnant without even touching her?"

That sounds like a question for Mr. Girouard.

(June 19, 1986)

AMAZING INVENTIONS TO COME

Trevor Beresford-Howe (not his real name) calls himself an environmentologist. What he means by the term is that he is an environmentalist who devises and implements "practical" solutions to some of today's numerous environmental problems.

The fact that Canadians currently rate the environment as the most pressing political issue means Mr. Beresford-Howe has a slightly more attentive audience these days. But his ideas are so outlandish, so plainly off-the-wall, that it's difficult to take anything he says seriously.

In a recent telephone conversation with Mr. Beresford-Howe from his home in Labrador, I asked him to elaborate on his proposed solution to the problem of non-biodegradable plastic bags that are clogging up the landfill sites of the nation.

"There's nothing much to elaborate on," Mr. Beresford-Howe said. "What we must do, quite simply, is switch to paper bags. They break down much more quickly than plastic bags, and can be used in all kinds of different ways."

I stifled a guffaw. "When you say paper, what exactly do you mean?"

"I mean paper," Mr. Beresford-Howe said. "*Paper* paper. A sufficiently rough bond could make an even more durable bag than the petroleum byproduct we use nowadays."

You can well imagine my disbelief.

Of all his outrageous notions, Mr. Beresford-Howe's thoughts on disposable diapers are probably the most loopy. With recent estimates that North American families go through roughly 20 billion disposable diapers per annum, adding up to some four million tonnes of garbage, and that it takes a disposable diaper roughly 500 years to decompose, the time is ripe for new ideas about diapers. But Mr. Beresford-Howe's proposal verges on the nonsensical.

"What we need are re-usable diapers," he said. "If a diaper were made of a durable natural fabric such as cotton, it could be used on the baby, laundered and used again and again, many times over."

"You're suggesting that the same diaper be used on an infant more than once?" I asked incredulously.

"Of course," Mr. Beresford-Howe said. "This, along with my paper-bag proposition, would go a long way toward resolving the current landfill crisis. I realize these ideas take some time to get used to, but time is unfortunately not a luxury at our disposal. We need revolutionary ideas and we need them now."

Diapers made of cloth: I tried to keep from laughing out loud at the concept.

"Are you sure your idea is sanitary?" I inquired.

"The department of health would have to do some scrupulous testing, but I'm convinced that with the help of all the sophisticated technology at our disposal, we can design and develop a fully reusable diaper. It's a scientific breakthrough that's just around the corner."

"You really think so?"

"I do," said Mr. Beresford-Howe. "We were able to land men on the moon 20 years ago, weren't we?"

Is Trevor Beresford-Howe (not his real name) a crackpot, a visionary or some strange combination of the two? That's for you to decide.

His radical ideas on environmental issues have already earned him the wrath of large and powerful corporations such as Dallas-based Kimberley-Clark, which controls one-third of the $84-billion American market for disposable diapers.

Researchers at Kimberley-Clark have spent the past five years designing and perfecting disposable training pants for the estimated four million children who will begin toilet training each year. The less the executives of this corporation hear about Mr. Beresford-Howe and his futuristic ideas, the happier they are.

But Mr. Beresford-Howe is undaunted. Lately he has ventured into the field of home gardening. One of his recent proposals is that instead of using chemical herbicides that have a potentially deleterious effect on the surrounding ecosystem, gardeners should consider manually uprooting weeds from their lawns and gardens.

"By hand," I said.

"Exactly. It can be surprisingly effective, not to mention invigorating. The weeds themselves can then be composted along with the lawn cuttings."

"You mean bending down and physically pulling the weeds out of the soil?"

"I do," Mr. Beresford-Howe said.

"That would take some getting used to," I said by way of understatement.

"I realize that," Mr. Beresford-Howe said. "So did the wheel, and electricity. All truly revolutionary concepts take time to sink into the mainstream of public consciousness. But that mustn't stop people like me from pursuing our research. For example, right now I'm working on the prototype for a pollution-free vehicle that could be powered by a domestic animal such as a horse or a team of dogs."

I could no longer suppress my laughter.

"Scoff if you wish," Mr. Beresford-Howe said, "but it doesn't stop the future from getting a little closer to the present every day."

He may have a point there.

(July 15, 1989)

THE POWER OF AUTO-SUGGESTION

The U.S. insurance industry has released another one of those indispensable reports that tells us large cars are generally safer to crash in than small cars.

The same profound revelation surfaced decades ago with the development of the tank as a useful way of motoring around in a war. Put enough steel between yourself and the rest of the world and you may live to tell the tale. But I'm quibbling.

The insurance industry's Highway Loss Data Institute says that among small cars, the Mercedes-Benz 380 SL and the Chevrolet Corvette are "substantially better than average" in terms of how little you're injured if you happen to hit something with it.

If it weren't for the fact that the Mercedes-Benz 380 SL and the Chevrolet Corvette cost somewhat more than a used Mini-Morris, this news would probably do wonders for their sales figures.

But bigness isn't everything: A less titanic *Titanic* might have been able to swerve safely around that iceberg in the North Atlantic. A sub-compact can turn on a dime, but you need a mortgage to do the same manoeuvre with an Oldsmobile.

I am not a total stranger to big cars. I once inherited, through marriage, a giant Pontiac equipped with gaping holes in the floorboard for Flintstone-style foot locomotion if the engine happened to quit – which it did on a regular basis.

My daughter always enjoyed watching the asphalt zoom by through the floor when we went on long trips in the Pontiac. I called the floorboard holes "passive climate control", until my wife decided to put pieces of wood over them; then they became "natural walnut finish underbody reinforcement".

One year, we decided the Pontiac could use a little body work. A friend, who lived in the country, volunteered to do it cheap. He substituted smart wood trim for the rusted chrome trim (to follow the styling theme we had established for the floorboard). And he reupholstered the seats in blue corduroy that looked to have been acquired from a used-clothing store.

The car didn't handle any better on wet pavement after all that restoration. But it did turn a few heads (or stomachs, depending on how you respond to wood trim and used corduroy upholstery).

Thank goodness our giant Pontiac never underwent the Highway Loss Data Institute's accident test. It might have thrown their theory out of whack.

I bought my all-time favourite car in 1977 for the princely sum of $600. Suffice to say it was a two-door, four-cylinder Japanese import. The previous owner raced four-cylinder imports in his spare time, so the machine had pep to spare, so he said.

Sure enough, it did. Unfortunately, as was so often the case with Japanese imports in the primitive '70s, the engine was willing but the body was weak. One day, the Highway Loss Data Institute's carefully-gleaned conclusions about the benefit of big cars were driven home to me -- literally.

The accident happened suddenly, as all accidents have a habit of doing. The woman driving the car in front of me braked to avoid a little brown dog that had wandered onto the road. We were both doing about 5 miles per hour. Either she braked too abruptly or I braked too late. At any rate, my car collided with the rear of her car. The entire right side of my car fell off with an enormous clang.

So frightened was the woman by the devastation that she sped away, leaving me to ponder that big chunk of my car leaning ingloriously against the curb.

The investigating officer tried to maintain his composure. "I think what you better do is take whatever's left of your car home," he finally said, giggling like a schoolgirl.

As I drove what was left of my car home, to the delight of pedestrians and motorists alike, I marvelled at how little of a car you really need in order to drive it. But I also pondered what might have been left of me had I been driving 50 miles per hour at the time of the accident.

This was how I came to be a defensive driver.

Defensive driving makes sense. And it's simple. All you have to do is assume that everybody else on the road, regardless of race, creed, colour or car size, is criminally insane.

Having done a fair deal of mid-winter driving in Ontario, I know for a fact that this assumption is not far off the mark. From December to April, the Queen Elizabeth Way should be renamed the Psycho Path.

(August 25, 1985)

12.

NOSTALGIA ISN'T WHAT IT USED TO BE

THE GREATEST WEEKEND OF THE YEAR

My most vivid Good Friday memory is of punting a football back and forth across an empty schoolyard with my friend Mike. The sky was almost unnaturally blue and the neighbourhood was perfectly quiet.

Neither Mike nor myself made a big deal about it at the time. I was 10, he was a bit older. We kicked a football around that day because we had the schoolyard to ourselves, the weather was ideal and girls bugged us.

We didn't say much while we played, but my pores and my eyes and my brain and my soul must have been raving about the mood of the morning for the memory to have survived this long. Nobody told us playing football might not be the most appropriate way of observing Good Friday.

Mind you, we did our playing in the morning and went to church precisely at mid-afternoon, not long after the last bird had given up singing. It was the time of year in the liturgical calendar when the Gospel overshadowed the rest of the ceremony, and the epic telling of the Passion story engrossed me, though we were made to stand throughout it.

One year, a group of men in the congregation took it upon themselves to sing the entire Passion, acappella. That made a definite impression on me – in part because we barely got home from church in time for supper.

But of all the cathedrals and ways of worship I've seen in the world, a spring sky and children at play still have the deepest meaning for me. Good Friday is the arc of a football against a ceiling of deep blue. I can't help it. I don't think I wan't to help it.

* * *

When I was a kid, the Easter weekend meant spring. Those years when Easter came in March, I had to stretch my imagination to conjure spring, but the lilies and palm fronds in the house helped the illusion along.

We didn't get into egg-painting much at my house. I and my brothers were usually presented with a hollow chocolate animal, which we proceeded to eat until there was no more. Sometimes we ate too much too quickly and too consciously, and we were reprimanded. So I learned to quietly put the half-eaten chocolate animal away, where it stayed until one of my brothers found it and ate it for me.

What I liked to do most on Easter weekend when I was young was to take a walk into the woods, which are so strangely frail-looking in the absence of undergrowth and leaves. The smells are vivid at this time of year; last autumn's leaves are a thick, soggy carpet under your feet and the air is so pure you can drink it. If you wander into the middle of the bush, you can almost hear the planet patiently going about its resurrection.

Easter and spring mean the same thing. We can read thousands of words on the simple theme of redemption, and even as we read, buds are forming on the branches and life is sprouting from the ground. The process is so simple as to defy description.

But simplicity too often escapes us. We've been told we have dominion over nature. That's probably why we're so much less elegant and direct than nature, so dependent on concrete, conscious meaning for things that are actually lighter than air, processes that are as natural and uncontrived as the seasons.

Humility is the ability to recognize your own limitations. Humility is also the ability to periodically shut yourself off and become part of the silent, greater harmony that's always there.

In other words, Christ died so children could play peacefully.

(April 18, 1984)

THE TUG OF THE OLD SOD

Dennis Laverty spent his middle age living, working and prospering in England. He also spent it pining for his native Ireland.

So deeply ingrained was his nostalgia for the soil of his home that when Dennis moved back to the Ulster town of Ballymena with his English wife Ruth in the late 1970s, he couldn't shake the deep longing that had marked his years away from home.

"Ah, Ireland," Dennis sighed one afternoon in the summer of 1980, the first time I visited the island. Dennis was a born storyteller and had been regaling us with a few tales of his youth. It was as though his young man's heart had left Ireland and never come back.

There was no point in reminding him he was back in Ireland now, in a comfortable country home, with his wife and a ferocious dalmatian by the name of Mandy who terrorized everyone but Dennis, who obviously worshipped her.

What Dennis was sighing about were the lost years away from his home, away from the incomprehensible peace and equally incomprehensible violence of a land where tragic history covers everything like a layer of geological sediment.

Dennis Laverty's first cousin, Arthur Parke, also left Ireland as a young man. But like Dennis – probably like all the Irish who are scattered here and there in the world – he was never able to get the land out of his system.

In Canada, Arthur and his wife Renee raised three children, one of whom I married. All of them were born in Ireland but left when they were still young children.

Arthur pursued a career in the mining business and eventually became a partner in a mining engineering firm in Richmond Hill. He and his family frequently returned to Ireland to visit his mother Jeannie and numerous aunts, uncles, cousins and friends.

In 1983, Arthur underwent quadruple-bypass surgery. Within a year he had sold his shares in the mining company and retired back to Ireland, where he opened a flower shop in the seaside town of Portstewart.

Soon after his return, Arthur began to meet regularly with his childhood friends on a street corner in the village of Cullybackey. They become known as the Cullybackey boys. I imagine the 30 years Arthur spent in Canada began to fade from that point onward.

The second time I visited Ireland, in 1985, Jeannie was no longer there to welcome us with her warm, easy laughter. But her only son, Arthur, compensated by virtually confining us in his car, chauffering us from point to point.

So happy was he with his new life in Ireland that Arthur even leased part of a peat bog at the foot of Slemish Mountain where, one clear morning as we collected the water-sodden bricks for drying and eventual burning, we could see the sea off in the distance. But the work was so back-breaking that he eventually had to give it up.

Arthur wasn't one for singing the praises of Ireland in words. He knew the view of the Mull of Kintyre from a windswept clifftop on the Antrim coast, or the vista of County Down from halfway up one of the Mountains of Mourne, would do all his talking for him.

He was right. I, like those who were born there, am now infected by this land.

The tug of the old sod on the hearts and minds of her scattered sons and daughters is strongest this weekend. On St. Patrick's Day, everyone who wants to can share in that power.

The last time I saw Ireland, it was to bury Arthur. By then, Dennis Laverty was gone, too, safely sheltered in the soil of his beloved land.

The day after Arthur's funeral, while stopping off at the market for fresh soda bread, we ran into a few of Arthur's old streetcorner chums. I don't remember what we talked about, but at one point in the conversation one of the men turned to me and said "This fella's a Cullybackey boy."

I haven't accumulated very many official titles in the course of my life, but "Cullybackey boy" is one I carry around with great pride.

(March 16, 1991)

WHEN MOVIES RAN ALL DAY

Last Saturday morning, I trooped downtown with an army of children to attend an event that's a rarity nowadays but was as common as cod liver oil in my youth: the Saturday morning movie matinee.

This particular matinee was even more of a rarity, in that the admission and the popcorn and the pop were free. In my day, a popcorn and a pop ran you upwards of 35 cents – a heavy financial burden when you consider that you had to fork over a quarter at the box office just to get in.

I have a theory about why the food and drink were gratis at this matinee at the Century cinema: I think the people who organized it believed this show of generosity and goodwill would shame any spirited kid out of the idea of flinging popcorn boxes at the screen and otherwise undermining the proceedings.

But then it occurred to me that popcorn no longer comes in boxes that neatly fold into square frisbees. One theatre chain serves popcorn in heavy-duty paper bags. The other chain serves it in a deep, round, cardboard container.

So imagine my surprise last Saturday morning when, upon queuing up at the concession stand with all the other kids, I saw that we were being handed little yellow boxes of popcorn.

O what delicious nostalgia for the days of my unspent youth!

* * *

Every summer for a couple of weeks, my cousin Mark would visit me in North Bay from his home in the small Ontario Hydro colony town of Rolphton, on the Ottawa River. Mark was four years younger than I but we were nonetheless kindred spirits.

We both enjoyed playing endless games of pinball at Demarco's Confectionary. We both liked to go to the Scollard Hall field and get the autographs of key Hamilton Tiger-Cats such as Bernie Faloney and Angelo Mosca when the Ticats held their training camp there. (My cousin and I were both Ottawa Rough Rider fans at the time, but those were the days when CFL stars were national celebrities.)

But above all else, my cousin and I loved to line up outside the Bay Theatre at the crack of dawn on Saturday mornings to while away a few of those seemingly infinite hours of childhood in the company of the Three Stooges and whatever obscure double-feature happened to be playing.

The Bay Theatre was long, narrow and excessively dark. The head usherette, who was about 115 years old, wielded a dim flashlight, but she could cover every inch of those aisle with her eyes closed. She was tough on misbehavers, but that just made her more of a challenge to a lot of kids.

My cousin didn't mind at all that the floor of the Bay Theatre consisted of a semi-permanent veneer of vulcanized cola syrup and chocolate that welded like super-velcro to the soles of our running shoes. To him the Bay was a place for urban sophisticates. His only other experience of a movie theatre was in the town of Rapides des Joachims, across the Ottawa River from Rolphton, where a supremely cross old man showed dinosaur epics in a church basement to a weekly audience of kids in fold-out chairs.

If the kids watching the dinosaur movie were doing too much talking and kibitzing, the man would stop the projector and bellow the word "SILENCE!!!" over and over again until he was satisfied.

My cousin and I liked to watch movies over and over again. In the summer of 1964, we saw *A Hard Day's Night* six times within a week. Three of those six times occurred during a memorable Saturday when the Beatles' movie was paired with *Fate Is The Hunter*, a sort-of mystery thriller starring Glenn Ford.

We arrived at the Bay Theatre at about 11 that Saturday morning. We left around 8:30 in the evening, when my mother showed up at the theatre in a state of profound perturbation. Having watched two movies, three times each, continuously for about nine hours, we had trouble grasping intellectually what she was upset about.

* * *

Nowadays, theatres do just about everything in their power to keep kids from watching movies over and over again on a single admission ticket. And the ushers tend to be younger and more fleet of foot, thereby deterring the popcorn-box storms and other movie-going rituals I remember so well.

The crowd that attended last Saturday's matinee was shockingly well behaved. Santa Claus paid a visit, the goodies were free, there was a movie poster, and kids who were brave enough to go up to the front and sing a Christmas carol were rewarded with nice prizes, from cases of pop to a toboggan.

In the old days at the Bay Theatre, my cousin and I and all the other kids had to make our own fun. If, one morning around Christmas, Santa had come walking down the aisle carrying a sack of pop and a brand-new, full-sized toboggan, I believe we would have been struck speechless and prankless – neutralized by all that goodwill.

(December 16, 1987)

RELIVING CHILDHOOD TO SCALE

None of the recently-cut VIA Rail routes were immortalized in elaborate miniature layouts at the enormous model-train show in Toronto last weekend.

But I did spot a handful of those distinctive gleaming silver *Canadian* passenger coaches for sale in individual packages, as though the federal government had zapped that now-defunct train with a shrinking ray and put in on the selling block in the more portable HO scale.

There's a distinct romance about beautifully detailed miniature railway equipment and infrastructure that seduces more than just children and hard-core hobbyists. Anyone who has spent more than a couple of weeks of their life within earshot of the evocative whistle of a long night train or the vivid smells and sounds of railway yards can't help but fall under the spell.

The model-train crowd's meticulous recreation of this environment occurs on a much, much smaller scale. But the romance of it all is not diminished in any way. In fact, the element of magic in this little world seems to heighten the sheer poetry of trains.

Why are trains poetic in the first place, one wonders? Why not buses, airplanes or even the ubiquitous automobile? What is it about these lumbering conveyors of goods and people that seems to have gotten under our collective skin and stayed there, while other modes of transportation have never penetrated deeper than the outer shell of our imagination?

The spell is an uncanny one, judging by the captivated throng at the model-train show. Even a child of the '90s, standing by a crude oval layout of HO tracks as a six-car train choogles 'round and 'round, is reduced to a calm silence in ways that the grandest Nintendo game or most ingenious remote-control monster truck is incapable of doing.

* * *

Model trains have been in my family almost as long as trains themselves. It may say something about the peculiar qualities of the romance of the rails that my grandfather, who retired from the Canadian Pacific Railway with a lifetime pass, vowed never to set foot on a train for the rest of his life. He kept his vow, to the best of my knowledge.

My grandfather regularly took my older brothers to the railway yards on weekends to watch the steam locomotives shunting to and fro. By the time he retired, diesel locomotives had all but replaced steam and my brothers were old enough to loiter down at the tracks by themselves, which was probably fine by him.

I vaguely recall a model-train layout in the basement of my childhood home. Much more vivid, though, is a long-festering allegation that a young cousin and I somehow "wrecked" that layout in a surfeit of youthful enthusiasm and/or mischief. (With those kind of credentials as a child, I might have made a top-notch federal minister of transport).

What I remember best about our basement layout – more even than the model train or the nicely landscaped layout through which it snaked – was the line of small brown plastic hydro poles alongside the tracks. You could almost imagine a flock of summer birds congregating on the wires in the early evening.

What I think I learned from my grandfather and from the dim memories of our basement layout is that the romance of trains is most palpable when you're standing still, watching the trains go by.

* * *

The romance of trains also stills time: There were one or two layouts at last Sunday's model-train show that showcased high-tech, high-speed trains, such as France's TGV *(Très Grande Vitesse)* or Japan's *Bullet*. But in most cases, a steam locomotive had the pride of place at the head of the train.

The mechanics of the model trains seem to have changed amazingly little in a generation, as though part of the way of keeping faith with the grand old trains is by tampering as little as possible with the way they're recreated on these small representations of the world through which they once rolled.

In my own small effort to keep the faith – and perhaps to atone for past misdeeds – I contributed quite a bit of HO-scale rolling stock and some tracks to my brother's planned layout before we set off for the model-train show.

It's a noble cause, this nailing down of a fragment of our past on a four-by-eight sheet of plywood.

(March 31, 1990)

WHEN THE MUSIC'S OVER

In our teens we tended to mark each passing Christmas with the records we received as presents and played and played and played right through to New Year's Day.

Twenty years ago, it was the White Album, the Beatles' double-record with the blank cover. It was as though, after toying with such colourful disguises as the Sergeant Pepper band, the Beatles had no collective identity left to present to the youth of the world, hence the untitled, white-as-a-snowstorm album.

Rick and I played the daylights out of that album, mainly on his parents' old hi-fi. Most of the 30 songs seemed to sum up something about our own lives. Looking back, we were no doubt projecting a lot of our own meanings onto the music, just as Charles Manson was doing.

Rick and I each received a copy of the White Album for Christmas. I played mine at home on loudspeakers my uncle had made for us.

Of all the pop music in those days, my mother was most tolerant of the Beatles. There was a particular song on the White Album that always made her laugh. Had she known its title – "Happiness Is A Warm Gun" – she might have thought otherwise. But what she found irresistibly funny was one of John Lennon's lines in the song: "Mother Superior jumped the gun." When Lennon sang that line, my mother chuckled.

I don't think I've ever asked her what she thought the line meant.

* * *

In those days, Rick and I drowned all the confusion, longing and dull sorrow of adolescence in music. He had an excellent reel-to-reel tape recorder. Together we made tapes of our own favourite records.

There was some discussion that year of whether to include "Revolution 9", a long, rambling piece of electronic music from the White Album, on our tape. The same debate was going on elsewhere. I remember sitting in the numbingly cold front porch of our house, amid the smell of dozens of *tourtières* stacked in natural refrigeration, listening to a radio DJ play "Revolution 9" and ask listeners what they thought of it.

I was listening to the radio in the frigid porch because I was waiting for a ride to the Christmas dance. My date for the night was the older sister of a girl who had asked me to the Halloween dance. (My diplomatic skills with the female sex were non-existent in those days. Girls were as alien to me as, well, aliens.) The DJ invited listeners to call and tell him what they thought of "Revolution 9." What a different time it was then: innocent, open-minded, naively experimental, naturally rebellious, and always with a strange something in the air – a spirit we kids silently understood and groped toward.

Rick and I finally decided to leave "Revolution 9" off the tape, mainly because it was too boring. Maybe if we had known that Lennon had only twelve years left to live, we would have listened more closely. Maybe not.

* * *

One evening late in 1968, lost in one of those weird collective teenage funks, Rick and I shut off the music and just stared out the window. It was a windless night. Snow was falling gently, slowly. We decided to go for a walk in it.

Snow falling on a windless night mutes the world. Cars move silently by. The snow in the sky and on the ground gives a grey glow to the darkness.

We walked mostly in silence, a couple of profane kids on a sacred night. We were lost in a moment in time, and it was leaving its mark on us.

I haven't seen or spoken to Rick in years, but I'm sure he remembers that night as vividly as I do.

Two years later, for Christmas 1970, I received a George Harrison album called All *Things Must Pass*. It was a grand, wistful valedictory album. Harrison seemed to be speaking directly to us and to the waning adolescence of our generation.

A few weeks later, on one of those bright and still February days, I attended my grandfather's funeral. That afternoon, I retreated to my room, plugged headphones into Rick's tape recorder and lost myself in the sad, sweet saxophone of Paul Desmond. The song he played most sweetly was called "So Long, Frank Lloyd Wright".

The music never sounded as serene as it did that day. That's because I was working as hard at it as Paul Desmond was, trying somehow to graft countless memories of life with my grandfather onto a few saxophone riffs.

From the vantage point of Christmas Eve 1988, it's impossible to tell where the music ends and the memories begin. That's probably a good thing.

But I also remember, in a deeper way, where I was when my grandfather died: out in the middle of a white windswept lake with Rick and a group of other classmates who had skipped school together that afternoon. The icy plain was perfectly soundless. It compelled all the music that was playing in our head to be still.

When all is said and done, the only thing more sacred than music is silence.

(December 24, 1988)

13.

NOW LET US GIVE THANKS

A LESSON IN LIFE

My room at St. Joseph's had a nice view of the north end of town, to the foot of the bay and across to Burlington and beyond. I didn't have the window bed; my roommate got there first. But neither he nor his loved ones minded if I went over to gaze out at the ideal view below me.

I say ideal because who, after all, wants to be in a hospital looking out? The world looks almost impossibly beautiful when you no longer have access to it.

I was in for elective surgery – an attempt to improve my ability to breathe. My roommate had no choice in the matter. Every breath he took seemed to entail an exercise of will as much as of lungs.

My roommate's lungs were in serious trouble. The shock of it was clearly etched on his wife's face. All the hospital could do with him was to keep him comfortable. Regularly, a nurse injected a syringe full of morphine into the intravenous sac hanging from a post at the foot of his bed. His cancer was inoperable.

"He hasn't had much of a retirement," his wife said, without bitterness. Not long after retiring, he had a heart attack. And now this. She told me you have no choice but to "put your faith in the man upstairs."

And yet, she said softly after a period of silent reflection, you wonder sometimes what it's all about.

My roommate wasn't privy to his wife's emotion. It was all he could do to make his devastated lungs process oxygen.

Getting into my baby-blue pyjamas that afternoon, I felt about as irrelevant and in the way as I've ever felt in my life.

* * *

Anyone who's been admitted to hospital for elective surgery knows the silly sensation of lounging in a hospital bed while in a state of demonstrably good health. The nurse told me I should do so anyway, for when the people came to take my blood, and so on.

My roommate had on a special surgical gown, which I would be forced to wear the following morning. I guessed they had put the gown on him for chemotherapy a few days before. He had no need for pyjamas or a housecoat. He wasn't going anywhere. His day, that sunny, ideal Tuesday afternoon, consisted of drifting in and out of a morphine haze, recognizing cherished ones, breathing a few barely comprehensible words, then lapsing back into sleep.

Late that evening, after someone had taken my blood and the anesthetist had asked me all the things he needed to know, after visiting hours were over and a kind of ambivalent calm had enveloped the hospital, a nurse came by and spent a few minutes alone at bedside with my roommate. His breathing had worsened, and he was moaning a lot.

What the nurse did was sit with him and hold his hand. What the nurse did was care for him, care about him.

* * *

As I was wheeled into the operating room the following morning, my greatest fear was that the general anesthetic would be too specific, that I'd be forced to watch the operation like everyone else in the room.

I was about to convey my fear to one of the attendants when I found myself being wheeled back to my room with a strange sensation – or lack of it – in the nasal area. The operation was over.

In the late afternoon, my wife and daughter came to visit. They wound up staring at me lying there, trying in vain to keep my eyes open. Someone brought supper on a tray: a jar of juice and a jar of strong coffee. I didn't budge. I was content to dine on cream of IV soup.

The next day, I told my roommate's wife he had passed a peaceful night. I immediately saw pain cloud her face. There was little consolation for her in such peace. She had just spent more than five hours at her husband's bedside, waiting in vain for him to surface, if only for a moment, from the unconsciousness into which he had slipped the day before. She might have said to him "Fight, darling. Fight, even if it hurts."

That evening, after his wife had left on her lonely drive home, my roommate woke up briefly. He called his wife's name a number of times. I think he did so as much out of concern for her as for himself. (This, I see now, is part of what a lifetime love is about.)

I got out of bed and went over to him. I will always remember his eyes, or what I saw in them: confusion, pain, determination such as I can only imagine, and fear. He mumbled something. I told him

I couldn't make it out. He said it again. I told him I would call a nurse if he needed one. He stared up at the ceiling and was silent. I uselessly climbed back into my bed, three feet away from him.

At this proximity, at this moment in his life and mine, how could we not be at least friends, if not brothers, or father and son? I had shared such moments with no one else in my life.

* * *

On Friday night around eleven, the hospital telephoned my roommate's family and told them to come quickly.

Their arrival didn't surprise me. His breathing had become shallower and even more terribly laboured that evening. He was deeply unconscious now. The only evidence of his tenacity was the sheer regularity of those tortured breaths. Despite everything, he was going to fight to stay alive until it was no longer feasible.

As his family gathered around his bed in the pale hallway light, I had no idea what to do with myself. Would it be unimaginably rude to pretend I was asleep, or even more unimaginably rude to lie there awake and intrude on another family's death vigil? Seventy-two hours ago, after all, we had been perfect strangers to one another.

I listened to my roommate's wife, son and daughter talk to him in tones of intimacy, affection and loss that will stay with me forever. Sometime during that long and awesome night, it came clear that a person's death is essential to life.

To be properly understood, sentences need punctuation – commas and periods. Without them, thoughts would run on and be meaningless. In the same way, death punctuates life, gives it meaning.

It occurred to me that if you've shared your life with someone, you're awfully lucky if you can share that person's death. And perhaps understand it.

* * *

My roommate didn't die that Friday night. His exhausted family reluctantly left the hospital for some sleep at mid-morning.

At 11, I was released from hospital. I felt as strange in my jeans as I had in my pyjamas four long days before. My wife picked me up. I said 'bye to my unconscious roommate and to the nurses, the golden nurses of the fifth floor. I took one last look at the view of the bay from that room.

The next day, Henry, my roommate, died. His name was among thirty-four others in the Death Notices in the paper.

I'm glad he didn't go while I was there, next to him. I wouldn't have deserved such a privilege.

As it is, I feel honoured to have been a temporary member of his family – to have had a precious education in how good people cope with a very great loss.

(May 20, 1987)

CARRICKFERGUS

He was born in New Brunswick, and named after a town in Ireland. I always got the sense of sea air and open spaces about him, though I don't suppose he ever spent time on an ocean beach.

The Irish town is Carrickfergus, whose old Norman castle overlooks Belfast Lough and the Irish Sea. The castle is a benign presence now, the site of a military museum and some well-kept ruins. People who live in Carrickfergus call it Carrick for short.

Carrick was the runt, and probably wouldn't have survived his mother's instinctive concern for the more fit of the litter if human hands hadn't intervened. So life was serendipity for him from birth –a bonus he had no right to count on. His habit of eating with total abandon is one he came by honestly. The runt of the litter literally doesn't know where his next meal is coming from.

Carrick wasn't a glutton, he was a survivor – though I'm not sure what would have happened had we ever set down a week's worth of food in front of him. In dogs as in humans, the survival instinct can be the root of some bad habits, especially when survival has long ago ceased to be an issue.

"Beasts abstract not," said a 17th century philosopher named Descartes. His declaration pleased his fellow human beings to no end, and it still pleases a lot of us. By concluding that all animals except humans were incapable of thought, Descartes' view of nature solidified the moral correctness of our position as master over nature.

Anyone who has the privilege of sharing life with a pet knows that Descartes had it all wrong. Dogs, cats, hamsters, rabbits, etc. may be incapable of the kind of "higher" reasoning for which *homo sapiens* is famous, but they possess a full-blown natural wisdom our elaborate consciousness can grasp only in momentary fragments. (We're at our best when we do grasp it.)

I loved to watch Carrick as he dreamed, lying in utter security on his back on the couch upstairs, his legs splayed comically in the air, his eyes darting under their lids. We assumed he was dreaming of running – it was his favourite activity, next to eating – because his legs would dance in an upside-down approximation of the chase. Perhaps he was running with Shannon, the little dog who became his adoptive mother and was a constant companion for ten of his fourteen years until she died tragically under the wheels of a car.

Carrick at full speed, in his prime, was something to behold – the noble mutt as a picture of grace.

It didn't surprise us that Carrick dreamed of running, or even that he dreamed. He seemed to spend a good deal of his life pondering imagined things: the eternal prospect of a scrap from the supper table; how to solve the gate at the side of the house; where the best garbage in the neighbourhood was; what bark to use when he wanted back in the house. This dog abstracted all the time, even in his sleep.

But for all his cleverness and his Houdini-like ability to bust out of fenced yards, Carrick never lost the heart of a puppy. He didn't have a jaded bone in his body. He was an innocent – a pure soul.

Four springs ago, we took Carrick on the first of a series of visits to his favourite place: the Royal Botanical Gardens arboretum. He dashed madly this way and that through the gully, as if the sights and scents of that glorious, muddy gorge had overloaded his circuits. Every now and then he'd run by us as a form of greeting, his tongue dangling from the side of his mouth, then bolt back into the woods.

He was so happy we could taste it. That's why we were so lucky to be with him.

Unless you're a pet owner, it's hard to appreciate the subtlety and depth of a relationship a human can have with a dog or cat. Sure, we're often guilty of projecting human motives and behaviour onto our pets. But the simple truth is we all have more in common with these animals than we'd like to admit.

Cats and dogs possess a highly refined sense of personal dignity. If they're wounded or in pain, they usually wander off to be by themselves. When he was five, Carrick was mauled by a Doberman. We had a terrible time getting him to a vet. He wouldn't come out from his dark shelter under a table.

Yet a few days ago, when he began to lose his race against time, Carrick sought us out. He spent the last day of his life in the backyard with us, lying more quietly than usual under a lawnchair in the benevolent April sun.

That evening, when I served him his food, he perked up and wolfed it down in his usual record time. But he became quiet again in the evening.

The next morning, it was clear he was in a lot of pain. Our uppermost wish was that the pain end.

After my daughter promised him she'd take him one day for a walk around the whole world, we drove Carrick to the vet's office. We spent a few moments alone with him there, saying our last goodbyes. I took his head into my hands, looked into his gentle eyes and whispered, "Go find Shannon."

It was an instruction to find his old and dearest friend, and to drift peacefully down the Irish river of that name until he reaches the great embracing sea.

(April 20, 1988)

HAPPINESS IS

I can't think of a better time of year to celebrate Thanksgiving Day than right now, on the heels of a long and fruitful summer.

The American version of the holiday, which falls on the fourth Thursday of November, arrives so deep into the most hopeless month of the year that it's hard to imagine anyone can muster the spirit to properly dissect a turkey, let alone give comprehensive thanks for the various blessings of life.

But right now, in the bright fresh days of October, gratitude seems almost reflexive. So here, with apologies in advance, is a random catalogue of things for which I personally feel grateful.

* The subtle onset of umber, orange, yellow, burgundy in the foliage of the Niagara Escarpment at this time of year.
* Microwave ovens. They help save us from our overly hectic lifestyles.
* The people who take away the garbage every week. If only there were some way of being reminded that just because the stuff leaves our front yard doesn't mean it disappears altogether.
* A warm bed in the middle of a cool night.
* Green-grey Lake Erie on a bright blustery autumn day.
* Fast-forward buttons on VCRs.
* The deepening blue skies and crisper light of autumn, even if they are the harbinger of the leaden overcast skies of November.
* Pumpkins, particularly the annual profusion of them outside Bennett's market in Ancaster.
* Neighbourhood businesses: commerce in user-friendly proportions.
* Three square meals a day – still a minority privilege on this planet.
* Indoor plumbing. As someone who recently suffered through a disastrous disruption of service (but that's another column), I have come to love the sound of hot and cold water flowing easily through the circulatory system of my house.
* Waiting for the first snow, which is a lot more fun than waiting for the last snow.

* The smell of fresh-made Colombian coffee.
* Wood heat.
* Four-season radial tires.
* Mikhail Gorbachev.
* Word processors.
* Primo pasta.
* My family (I should point out here that the order of this list is neither alphabetical nor of relative importance. All relatives are important to me, and I wouldn't be writing this if it weren't for the alphabet.)
* The moon.
* The Montreal Expos, for reasons that elude me by the middle of each summer.
* The gradual demise of digital watches.
* Turkey stuffing, which is the raison d'etre of the turkey. Ditto tangy homemade cranberry sauce.
* Andrei Tarkovsky.
* Telephone answering machines, now that I have one.
* Lazy late Sunday afternoons of half-watched football games on television as darkness falls slowly and imperceptibly.
* Halloween caramel kisses, wrapped in a waxy orange and black, and the sudden memories they inspire of youthful anticipation and excitement.
* The craving for junk food, always more interesting than junk food itself.
* Housepets – cats, dogs, rabbits, hamsters, boa constrictors – who only ask for a reasonably regular food supply and some affection. They always give more than they get.
* New potatoes.
* Butter.
* Van Morrison.
* The eastern sky at dawn.
* The western sky at dusk.
* The northern sky in the middle of the night.
* James Joyce.
* The perfect heft of a ripe, garden-grown beefsteak tomato in the palm of one's hand.
* The opportunity to be thankful.
* The Big Dipper, crossing the night sky like an automated ladle.

* The tiny staccato steps of trotting cats. (They seem so purposeful precisely because their lives are the model of simplicity.)
* The colour of sumac leaves in October (the only word I can use to describe the colour is "October sumac").
* Cool sand on bare feet after the sun has set.
* Herbert von Karajan conducting Beethoven's Ninth Symphony and understanding every last bar of it.
* Patsy Cline, who knew how to hurt in a song.
* The soulful eyes of mongrel dogs, who love their masters madly, purely, indiscriminantely.
* The Band, because their music sounds as ancient now as it did when it came out in the late '60s and early '70s.
* Curry and saffron on a breast of chicken.
* Laurentian colouring pencils.
* A close ball game in late innings.
* Spaghetti carbonare.
* The tingle in the fresh air on the south shore of the St. Lawrence River in the middle of a summer holiday in the middle of life.
* Bacon in its various incarnations.
* Stephen Lewis, the only remotely political individual I can place in this list without reservation.
* The vast Canadian landscape, because it ignores our ignorance of it.
* The Group of Seven, who refused to ignore the Canadian landscape.
* Martin Scorsese.
* Handel's organ concertos.
* PBS and TVOntario, because they don't run *Jake And The Fatman* or Lindsay Wagner movies.
* Hound Dog Taylor and other senior-citizen blues artists.
* Waking up in the morning before the clock-radio comes on.
* Pressing the snooze button on the clock-radio after it comes on.
* Pressing the snooze button a second time.
* Christmas carols.
* Blue boxes, even if they just scratch the surface of our garbage.
* The smell of oil paint.

* Russian movies, because they never pander.
* Digital audio.
* UNICEF.
* Gerard Dépardieu, France's entertainment gift to the world.
* Georges Erasmus, who kept his cool even when he was boiling inside in the summer of Oka.
* Ray Charles.
* Poetry, always more of a prayer than a sales pitch.
* Anonymous donors.
* Fresh popcorn with no butter and a sprinkle of salt.
* You who have read this far.
* Nurses.
* The Caribbean Sea in mid-afternoon, poised on the brink of some new frontier of blue-green.
* Leonard Cohen, who has remained consistenly weary, thereby perking the rest of us up.
* A tent, a sleeping bag, and a starry sky like a dot-to-dot puzzle.
* Pure silence, which seems to be disappearing as quickly as the rain forests.
* My daughter's Sunday dinners.
* Jamaica's Olympic bobsled team, for being so seriously, resolutely daft.
* Artists who ignore commercial trends and are inspired by deeper motives.
* The unbelievably soft fur at the very tip of my cat's tail (if she had any sense at all she'd be a lot more vain about it.)
* Ontario's adventurous voters.
* Map-O-Spread (I haven't had it on toast in years, but I remember the taste and texture like it was yesterday).
* Impressionism.
* Flannel bedsheets.
* Campsite 20 at Finlayson Point Provincial Park in Temagami, in the shade of 200-year old cedars. Lay down your troubles there sometime.
* Boris Yeltsin, who might just be exactly what he says he is.
* The glens of Antrim , where I hope to walk before the year is out.
* The rustic, luminous art of Burlington's Gisele Comtois-Osgood.
* Evergreens in general, tamarack, and jack pine in particular.

* Fyodor Dostoyevsky, whose late 19th-century novels speak directly to our age.
* Coming upon a young fox on a wooded trail in Killarney Provincial Park. The fox stares expectantly at me, I stare expectantly back at the fox. Time stops.
* Book publishers in general, Mosaic Press in particular.
* The lavishly stocked classical music department of Hamilton's Sam the Record Man.
* Pure Irish honey – and my wife too.
* The precious, muted sunlight of late afternoon in winter.
* Mario Lemieux, who proved he's the Really Great One.
* French fries at the Arbor on a summer afternoon in Port Dover, and milkshakes at Hewitt's on the way home.
* Katherine Porter, who has taken her unique art to Ottawa but left generous portions of herself in Hamilton.
* Theo Angelopoulos, Greece's finest filmmaker.
* Afternoon naps, which beautifully suspend time for a moment or two, then release you and restore you. My best afternoon naps usually occur with music playing on headphones, like a dream sound-track.
* Mozart's clarinet concerto, performed by James Cambell and Ottawa's National Arts Centre Orchestra under Franz-Paul Decker. This is nap music *par excellence.*
* A campfire.
* The moving shadows of tree branches on a bare wall.
* Candlelight. Electric bulbs are more practical, but practicality has been overrated for centuries.
* The slow, majestic coloration of maple trees at this time of year.
* Doing nothing, which is not nearly as easy as doing something, and can be extremely rewarding in moderation.
* A June birthday breakfast amid the peonies, clematis and mock-orange.
* The John Laing Singers, one of Hamilton's best-kept secrets.
* Joseph Campbell, whose knowledge of world mythology and unique ability to convey that knowledge made life and the world more interesting.
* Pure garden tomato sauce on pasta.
* All the stars you can see when you get far enough away from the city on a clear night. No wonder I used to gaze up at them so much when I was a kid.

* Umberto Eco, for reminding us in *Foucault's Pendulum* that what we don't know will forever exceed what we know.
* My cousin Michael, who stunned us 10 years ago at my aunt's funeral by singing "Amazing Grace" with heart-breaking clarity and feeling. May peace find you, Michael.
* The Blue Jays, because they made my Uncle John happy.

(October, 1989, 1990, 1991)